Prairie Fire!

"Drover, snap out of it! Don't you get it? Smoke in the air means we're downwind from a prairie fire!"

His eyes grew as wide as two fried eggs. "Fire! Oh my gosh, I think I'll faint."

And before my very eyes, that's what he did, went over like a bicycle, just as a vehicle pulled into the gravel drive in front of the machine shed. I left Drover where he lay and rushed outside.

Loper jumped out of the pickup and yelled, "There's a fire on Parnell's! Saddle the horses, we've got to move the cows out of this pasture!"

On an ordinary day, Slim didn't move at dazzling speed, but this woke him up. He leaped to his feet and gazed off to the south, where a big column of angry white smoke was rising in the air.

"Good honk!"

"Looks like the wind's taking it east of the house, but it's going to burn the home pasture. I'll call the fire department."

The Almost
Last Roundup

John R. Erickson

Illustrations by Gerald L. Holmes

Maverick Books, Inc.

MAVERICK BOOKS, INC.

Published by Maverick Books, Inc.

P.O. Box 549, Perryton, TX 79070

Phone: 806.435.7611

www.hankthecowdog.com

First published in the United States of America by Maverick Books, Inc. 2015.

1 3 5 7 9 10 8 6 4 2

LIBRARY OF CONGRESS CONTROL NUMBER: 2015931081

978-1-59188-165-0 (paperback); 978-1-59188-265-7 (hardcover)

Hank the Cowdog® is a registered trademark of John R. Erickson.

Printed in the United States of America

To my best students:
Mark Erickson,
Nathan Dahlstrom,
and Nikki Georgacakis.

CONTENTS

CHAPTER ONE

Hard Times

It's me again, Hank the Cowdog. On my ranch, we'd seen summers that were hot and summers that were dry, but we'd never seen anything like the kind of hot and dry we were going through in...whatever year it was.

We hadn't gotten much snow over the winter months, and we missed the spring rains that usually come in April and May. Then came the summer heat. Bad. Awful. Not just one or two blistering days every week, but day after day of temperatures over a hundred degrees, and a constant life-sucking wind out of the southwest.

Our hay field produced about half the number of bales it should have. Ponds dried up. Wolf Creek shrank down to a trickle. Pastures turned into burned toast. Cow trails grew deeper and dustier.

Trees were starting to die, and we're talking about native trees: hackberries, elms, cottonwoods, and even cedars. Fellers, when the cedars turn up their toes, you know you're in a bad drought, because those old cedars are tougher than boot leather.

We had no wildflowers that year, no mosquitoes, and very few grasshoppers. Even the birds quit us. You know me, I'm no fan of noisy birds, but for crying out loud, when all the birds moved out...I hate to admit this, but the ranch seemed kind of lonely without them.

This would have been a great time for a dog to take a vacation and go visit some place that had penguins and icebergs, but the Security Division gets no vacations and no days off.

That's where we were when the mystery began: roasted, toasted, hot, dehydrated, worn out, and wind-blown, and everybody on the ranch was on edge about prairie fires. See, when the pastures are bone dry and the wind is roaring, any little spark can start a blaze, and once it starts...I guess you'll find out.

I don't want to reveal too much, but...well, we had a fire. That comes later in the story, after I

rescued Sally May from the Charlie Monsters and after Little Alfred had smuggled something out of his mother's kitchen, but you're not supposed to know about any of that stuff, so don't tell anyone.

Sh-h-h-h-h.

Where were we? Oh yes, the drought.

The cowboys were sick of the heat and the dust, and disgusted that they were having to feed cattle in the summer. And boy, you talk about being in a foul mood! They weren't fit to be around. When they weren't complaining about the drought, they were snarling at each other, and when they got tired of that, they yelled at the dogs.

What were the dogs supposed to do about the drought? Actually, we tried a few home remedies. For three whole days in July, Drover and I stationed ourselves on a hill north of headquarters and barked at the clouds. They formed up into thunderheads, then fell apart and turned into fuzzy little do-nothing puffs that gave us about fifteen drops of rain.

Fifteen drops! We needed fifteen inches and we got fifteen drops. It was an outrage, a huge waste of time. If a cloud's too lazy and dumb to make a rain, there's nothing a dog can do about it.

4

When barking at the clouds didn't produce any results, we tried singing our "Drought Song." You're probably not familiar with that one. Good. That means you've never been locked in a drought that was so bad, you tried to sing your way out of it.

I don't suppose you'd want to hear it, would you? I mean, the subject matter is kind of depressing, but it's not a bad little song. Pretty good, in fact. Yes, by George, you need to hear it. Stand by to roll tape.

Drought Song

Desiccated gramma grass, wilting on the ground.
Crisp yellow leaves are falling all around.
A west wind blows with cruel might,
And the prairie fires burn all through the night.

> We need rain.
> We need rain.
> Not a cloud in the sky, in the pale blue sky.
> If we don't get a rain, everything is gonna die.

Dried up sage brush, looking mighty sad.
Chinaberry trees never saw it this bad.
Cottonwoods fade, showing barren limbs,
And the fish in the ponds are forgetting how to swim.

We need rain.
We need rain.
Not a cloud in the sky, in the pale blue sky.
If we don't get a rain, everything is gonna die.

The grass is gone, the hay's used up.
The cows look thin and they're hunting grub.
The people are tired and filled with doubt,
And the dogs are sick of this stinking drought.

We need rain.
We need rain.
Not a cloud in the sky, in the pale blue sky.
If we don't get a rain, everything is gonna die.

The people are tired and filled with doubt.
And the dogs are sick of this stinking drought.

So there you are, a pretty neat song about a bad subject. I wish I could report that it brought us a big rain, but it didn't.

But life goes on, doesn't it? In spite of the stinking drought, my day began in its normal fashion. I was up before daylight, staked out my usual position on that little hill north of headquarters, and barked up the sun.

Once I had that done, and while most people and dogs were still in their beds, I launched the Second Phase of my morning's routine, a complete and thorough walk-around of ranch headquarters. I checked it out from top to bottom: saddle shed, feed barn, machine shed, sick pen, garden, Emerald Pond, and every square inch of the corrals.

It took me two hours, and I saw no signs of the Charlie Monsters who showed up later and took Sally May as a hostage. I mean, those guys really caught us...

Wait. I wasn't supposed to say anything about that, so let's pretend that I didn't. I was misquoted, how does that sound? If anyone asks about the you-know-whats, we know nothing about them at this point in the story and have no comment for the press. I think that'll work.

Anyway, after two solid hours of pretty intense sniffing around, I was feeling tired and thirsty, and made a Water Stop at the stock tank in the corrals. As I stepped up on the cement apron, my eyes caught sight of something lying on the shady side of the tank.

I froze.

It had a beak, two eyes, and a wild shock of something red on top of its head. In certain

7

respects, it resembled a chicken or maybe a rooster, but I waited for Data Control to run Identity Scan. In my line of work, we have to be very cautious. Our enemies are clever and often use disguises, don't you see, and sometimes they come creeping into ranch headquarters, wearing chicken suits.

If this was an enemy agent in a chicken disguise, I needed to know about it.

A message clicked across the screen of my mind: "Carbon-based organism with feathers. Chicken. Male. Have a nice day."

I allowed myself to relax. It was J.T. Cluck, one of our local bird-brains, loafing in the shade, and I didn't want to waste half an hour of my life listening to him yap about whatever insignificant thoughts were floating through his little rooster mind.

I began backing away from the tank, in hopes that he might not have seen me. Too late. He cocked his head to the side and squawked, "Oh, there you are. It's about time you showed up."

"Sorry, J.T., I didn't mean to disturb you. I need to move along."

"Not so fast, mister. Every chicken on this ranch has been wanting to talk to you."

"I'm a busy dog."

"Yeah, I've noticed—busy sleeping. Every time I look around, you're spread out on that gunny sack bed, pumping out a line of Z's."

"Maybe you should find something else to do, besides snoop on me."

"It ain't snooping. Somebody needs to stay awake and pay attention."

"Are you finished?"

"No, as a matter of fact, I'm just getting cranked up." He stood up on his skinny legs and leaned closer to my face. "Pooch, we've got a crisis a-brewing on this ranch!"

CHAPTER TWO

Okie Dokie Doodle

W ell, I had been trapped into a conversation with J.T. Cluck, so I figured I might as well make the best of it and hear about the latest "crisis" on the ranch.

"Okay, talk, and try to skip the boring parts."

"Pooch, me and every chicken on this ranch want to know what you're going to do about this grasshopper shortage."

"I'm going to get a drink of water."

"Well, whoop-tee-doo. Listen, doggie, we ain't seen a grasshopper since last October. How's a chicken supposed to make a living around here?" I lapped water. "Course, you don't give a rip, 'cause they give you all that high-dollar grow-pup in a bowl. You might have a different attitude if you had to hustle your own grub."

"What are you complaining about? Sally May throws out grain for the chickens every morning."

"I know she does, but that stuff gives me heartburn."

I groaned. "Don't start the heartburn stories. I don't think I can stand it today."

He patted his chest and out came a ridiculous little chicken burp. "There, you see? I pecked that grain twenty-four hours ago and it's still giving me fits. Elsa says I need more gravel in my craw, but that ain't it. I need good old, honest American grasshoppers. A rooster can't make a living on stink bugs and scorpions. You ever eat a scorpion?"

"No."

"Well, you've never had heartburn 'til you eat one of them little heathens. Son, they'll bring tears to your eyes. They bite and sting all the way down the pipe. Why, the last time I ate a scorpion..."

"J.T., is there a point to this?"

"Huh? A point? Well, sure there is, and I'm a-getting there." He glanced over his shoulders and dropped his voice. "Pooch, I've been a-meaning to talk to you about this. Elsa thinks there's more to this grasshopper situation than meets the eye."

He waited for me to show some interest. "Are you going to listen to this or spend the rest of your life lapping water?"

I had drunk my fill, so I sat down beside him. "I'll give you five minutes."

"Well, this is important stuff and it might take longer than that."

"If it does, I'll get up and leave. Hurry up."

"All right, I'm a-hurrying." He leaned toward me. "Pooch, Elsa thinks she knows who's behind this grasshopper shortage. It's the British."

"Who?"

"The British. It's a plot. They're stealing us blind!"

I laughed. "That's ridiculous. We're in a drought. No rain, no grass, no grasshoppers. It's all about the weather."

He looked up at the sky. "Well, that's what all the smarties say, but some of us look a little deeper. And maybe you'd better do some checking on it yourself, since you're the guard dog around here."

I heaved a sigh. "Okay, who are the British?"

"That's where it gets a little hazy. We ain't entirely sure."

"Oh brother."

"But if you'll hush your mouth for a minute,

I'm a-coming to the best part of the story."

"Hurry up."

He rocked up and down on his toes, and stroked his chin with the tip of a wing. "Pooch, years ago when I was a little chickie, a storm come up from the northwest, big old storm, terrible storm, crash and boom, and I remember it like it happened yesterday. My granddaddy come into the chicken house, a-flapping and a-clucking, and I'll never forget the words he said."

He looked up at the sky. "He was a wonderful gentleman, and you know, he tried to warn me about eating scorpions and centipedes, but like a darned kid, I didn't pay him any mind, thought I knew everything, and I can trace my heartburn back to the very first time I ate a scorpion. Hadn't thought of that in years."

"He rushed into the chicken house. What did he say?"

"Huh? Oh, that. Yes, well, he come a-flapping into the chicken house and all of us little chickies was scared to death. There was a bunch of us in that hatch. I had thirteen brothers and sisters."

"What did he say?"

"Well, he come a-rushing inside and said, 'Y'all need to run around in circles and flap your wings

13

and cluck, 'cause the British are coming!' And since that day, in times of trouble, we run around in circles and yell, 'The British are coming!'"

I laughed. "I wondered how that got started."

"Well, there it is. It's a true story, and, mister, I think the British are here, and that's why we've run out of grasshoppers." He folded his wings across his chest and narrowed his eyes at me. "What do you say to that?"

"I'm glad you turned in the report, J.T.. I'll get right to work on it."

He was surprised. "Well, I didn't expect to hear that. You're actually going to investigate?"

"Oh yes, no question about it. This is serious stuff."

"It sure is if you're a chicken. How come you're grinning?"

"I enjoy my work. Can you give me a description?"

"Of what? Oh, the British? Let me think here." He stroked his beak and gazed off into the distance. "Granddad wasn't real clear on that. The best I can remember, he said they wore funny hats."

"On their heads?"

"Yes, on their heads. That's where most people wear their hats."

"I'm just checking, J.T., it's part of my job."

"That's fine, as long as you ain't poking fun."

"Oh no. Any other clues or details?"

"Let me think here. Oh yeah, one of them Britishers called himself Yokie Dandy Doodle. He was a general or something."

"Got it. What else?"

"Well, he went to town, riding on a donkey."

"Very interesting."

"There's more, it's a-coming back to me. He wore a feather in his cap and ate a macaroni sandwich."

"Macaroni sandwich, wow." I rose to my feet. "Excellent. I'll open a file on Okie Dokie Doodle and get started on the investigation right away. If he's been stealing grasshoppers, we'll get to the bottom of it."

J.T. held me in a searching gaze. "You know, pooch, all these years I've misjudged you. I never thought you had sense enough to walk across a road, but I admit that I'm kind of impressed."

"Thanks, J.T., impressing roosters is something I've always dreamed of doing."

"That makes me proud, sure does. Say, did I ever tell you about the time I ate one of them japaleena peppers? Boy, you talk about a fire in the engine room!"

"Some other time, J.T. I need to get to work on this case. See you around, and watch out for the British."

"Sure will, sure will. And you keep me informed, hear?"

"You bet."

I hurried away. Somehow I had managed to get through the conversation without laughing my head off.

Can you believe that conversation? The British were stealing grasshoppers, Yokie Dokie Doodle... what a bird-brain! And I was supposed to be protecting him from the Bad Guys. Sometimes I wonder...oh well.

So where were we? Oh yes, after being entertained by J.T. Cluck's heartburn stories, I headed down to the office, where I found some nice shade and two gunny sack beds. Drover was occupying one of them, conked out asleep, and I slid into the embrace of the other one.

Don't get me wrong, I didn't sleep. No sir, we have pretty strict rules about sleeping during business hours. I needed to conserve my energy, as well as catch up on reports and work out the schedule for Night Patrol. See, sometimes I do my paperwork in bed.

All of a sudden, I was awakened by a piercing...

Wait. Let me rephrase that. I wasn't asleep and therefore couldn't have been awakened by the scream. I was writing up my notes of the J.T. Cluck Comedy Hour, remember? Yes, that was it. The British were stealing his grasshoppers.

The Head of Ranch Security doesn't sleep in the middle of the day. Let's just say that upon hearing the awful scream, I leaped out of my office chair and took charge of the situation. "Parsley bubbles on the lumber bunny cobblers! Outrageous freckles see no evil and we shall beat to quarters!"

With jerky movements of my head, I glanced around and saw...what was that thing? It was mostly white. On one end, it seemed to have a head and on the other end, a stub of a tail. The creature stood on wobbly legs and stared at me with eyes that resembled...I don't know, two bowls of dishwater.

I beamed a merciless glare at the stranger and yelled, "Halt! Stop in the name of the lawn! Who goes there?"

A mysterious voice said, "Poppy hop along with pollywog jelly."

"That's your name? Let's see some ID, and keep all five feet on the ground."

"I thought I heard someone scream."

"Roger that. I heard it too, and we've got units checking it out, even as we squeak. What's your name? We need a name to go with the face."

"Which face?"

"The one you're wearing."

"Oh, that one." He blinked his eyes and gazed around. "Well, I guess I'm Drover. I wasn't sure at first, but I think I am."

"I've heard that name before."

"Yeah, I live here."

"Ah! Now we're getting somewhere. Your name must already be in our system, so form a line and pick up your uniform." I narrowed my eyes and looked closer at him. "Did you say your name is Drover?"

He grinned and nodded. "Yeah. Hi."

"Hello. We used to have a Drover on the staff and he drove me nuts. What are you, his cousin or something?"

"No, it was me all along. Sometimes they call me Rover, but it's Drover with a D."

"Drover with a D? Are you suggesting that I can't smell your name? And speaking of smell..." I moved closer and checked him out with Sniffatory Scanners. "I'm picking up a strange odor. Explain."

"Well, I rolled on a fresh cow pie."

"Why would you do that?"

He grinned and shrugged. "I don't know, it seemed like the right thing to do."

"It was the *wrong* thing to do. You stink. You said Drover, right?"

"Yeah, with a D."

"Please stop telling me how to spell your name. The point is that you're Drover with a D. We've known each other for a long time, which makes me wonder..." I glanced around in a full circle. "Where are we?"

"In our bedroom, under the gas tanks."

"Ah. That explains the *deja voodoo*, the feeling that I've been here before."

"Yeah, about a million times. We were asleep and something woke us up."

"I wasn't asleep. Who can sleep on this ranch? Even so...what do you suppose woke us up?"

His eyes grew large. "It was some kind of scream."

That word, "scream," seemed to activate all my professional instincts, and I knew we had a serious problem on the ranch. Just how serious, I didn't know. You don't either, so you'd better keep reading.

CHAPTER THREE

The Charlies Capture
Sally May

Okay, we had a problem. I began pacing, as I often do when I'm following a trail of clues. "It's coming back to me now. I heard a horrible scream. You heard it too?"

"Yeah, it was awful."

"It was a blurd-cuddling scream, right?"

"Oh yeah, it blurded my girdle."

"Did it come from a man, woman, or child?"

"I think so."

I stopped pacing and gave him a flaming glare. "Which one?"

"Well, I think it was a woman in distress."

"That's it! Sally May is in trouble and if we don't get there before it's too late, it'll be too late. Quick, Rover, it's time to launch all dogs!"

"It's Drover with a D."

The little mutt had picked up the habit of repeating, "It's Drover with a D." Why? Who knows? Maybe some of his brain cells had begun to rot from lack of use. He needed months of therapy, but I didn't have months to spare.

I leaped into the cockpit, dropped the canopy, and pushed the throttle lever all the way to Full Flames.

The roar of rocket engines filled my ears and I...I eased off on the throttle lever and cranked open the canopy. "Where are we going?"

Drover shrugged. "I don't know. Where'd the scream come from?"

"Well, yes, duh. That's the question. Give me coordinates."

"Which ones?"

"I don't care, but hurry up!"

"Well, let's see. Two-by-four, two-by-six, hole-in-one, and two eggs over-easy."

"Roger that. Thanks." I entered those numbers into the computer and was about to blast off, when I heard the scream again. "Wait. It's coming from the machine shed."

"Yeah, but Sally May never goes to the machine shed."

I leaped out of the cockpit. "Do you want to

save her life or argue about where she goes? Lock and load, son, we're going up the hill!"

Obviously the Charlies had captured the machine shed and somehow Sally May had walked into a trap. Now they were holding her hostage.

Our troops left the barracks and went racing up the hill, lugging full packs and extra ammo. The Charlies saw us coming and opened up with everything they had, but we didn't slow down or even blink an eye.

We had to take that hill and save Sally May.

Boy, you should have been there to see us. You talk about a couple of brave ranch dogs! Bullets zipped past our heads, then came mortar fire, tanks, RPGs, flame throwers, the whole nine yards of heavy combat.

Halfway up the hill, I sent Company B to cover the left flank, while I went plunging straight ahead. In serious combat situations, we put the slackers on the flanks. The Head of Ranch Security goes straight up the middle, with guns blazing.

And, fellers, my guns were blazing: bark after bark, roar upon roar, blast after blast of deep manly barking. I gave 'em everything I had: spray barking, mortar barks, canon barks, even a few deadly sniper barks.

Dodging enemy fire, I crested the top of the hill. There, I laid down another withering barrage of barking and yelled, "Security Division, Special Crimes Unit! Drop your weapons! Everyone on the ground! Move!"

Through the clouds of smoke and dust, I saw...hmm. I had expected to see dozens of Charlie commandos wearing vegetable-colored uniforms, and Sally May tied to a tree, only that wasn't the scene that presented itself before my very eyes. Instead, I saw...

Tell you what, we're going to cancel the Red Alert. Sit down and take a few deep breaths. See, we'd gotten some...some bogus information about this deal. What I saw in front of the machine shed was two men, and they weren't Charlie commandoes. I recognized them at once: High Loper, the owner of the ranch, and Slim Chance, the hired hand.

Loper seemed to be replacing a windshield wiper blade on his pickup, while Slim was seated on a five gallon bucket beside the stock trailer, and holding an air wrench that looked exactly like a fully automatic pistol, only it had a rubber air hose stuck in the bottom.

Perhaps he was working on the stock trailer.

Yes, that's what he was doing, pulling the tires off the right side of the trailer.

Those screams we'd heard? The air wrench. It made a horrible screeching sound, like a woman in distress.

Look, when you're Head of Ranch Security, you don't get a week or a month to respond to a crisis. Those crises come at us like bullets from all directions, and we make our best decision, based on the information at hand. It had been my bad luck that the initial Invasion Report had been filed by my assistant, Drover with a D.

But never mind. Slim Chance was pulling the tires off the stock trailer. He sat on an overturned five-gallon bucket and when I arrived on the scenery, he turned and gave me a scowl. "Quit barking. You're giving me a headache."

Quit barking? Headache? Oh brother.

You know what I did? *I barked at him*! Yes sir, I gave him a couple of big ones, just to let him know that, by George, when we have to send troops up the hill on a hot day, we're going to *bark* at something.

He rolled his eyes and shook his head, then spoke in a kinder tone of voice. "Hank, come here."

Okay, he was ready to make peace. Was I dog

enough to accept his apology? It was a tough call, but I decided...sure. I mean, a huge part of my job is figuring out how to get along with these people. When they mess up, we have to smooth things over and move on with our lives.

I flipped a couple of switches to disable the Firing Systems, and trotted over to him. He rubbed me on the ears and looked into my eyes. "Hank, have you ever had your tail unscrewed?"

Huh? Tail unscrewed?

He showed me the air wrench. "If you keep barking, I'll be forced to unscrew your tail. And if that don't work, I'll unscrew your nose."

He pulled the trigger and the wrench squealed.

I backed away. What kind of apology was THAT? All at once, I was overwhelmed by the realization that this cad didn't deserve a loyal dog. I whirled around, lifted my head to a proud angle, and marched away.

I hadn't gone far when I ran into Company B. He was out of breath. "Gosh, what happened? Where's Sally May?"

"Sally May isn't here. She was never here."

He glanced around. "Then...who screamed?"

Just then, Slim goosed the air wrench and it let out a screech. Drover grinned. "Oh, I get it now. It was the air wrench, right? Hee hee. Boy, he sure fooled us."

I glared into the emptiness of his eyes. "He fooled *you*. As a result, we launched an invasion force and put our troops in harm's way for nothing."

"Yeah, but there wasn't any harm. Nobody got hurt."

"What about the morale of this unit? Had you thought of that?"

"Well…"

"Of course you hadn't, so think about it. How can we continue to call ourselves the Elite Troops of the Security Division when we get involved in pointless, bonehead crusades?"

"Well…"

"It makes us look like morons, Drover. Is that what you want to be when you grow up, a little moron?"

"Can I scratch?"

"What?"

"I've got a flea on my left ear, and I sure need to scratch."

I could feel my eyes bulging out of their sprockets. "You will NOT scratch your left ear in the middle of my lecture."

"How about the right one?"

"No. Answer my question."

"I forgot. What was it?"

A great silence filled the silence. "I don't remember it either. You see what you've done to me?"

"Sorry."

I rummaged through the laundry basket of my memory. "It must have been important."

"I'll bet it was."

"But if it was so important, why can't we remember it? I mean, we're not just a couple of goofballs."

"Boy, that's right. Can I scratch now?"

"No, not until we remember the question that was before this court."

The silence grew deeper and heavier, then Drover said, "Maybe we could make up a new question."

"Why would we want to do that?"

"So I can scratch. This itch is killing me."

"Well, I guess we could. Sure. I mean, we can't spend the rest of our lives, just sitting here. Can you think of any good questions?"

"Well, let me see." He wadded up his face and squinted one eye. "Okay, here's one. If water runs downhill, how come it can't walk?"

"Because it has no legs."

"Then how can it run?"

"Drover, don't get started on this."

"A table has four legs, and it can't walk either."

"Tables have wooden legs."

"So do pirates, and they walk just fine."

I paced away from him and took several deep breaths of air. Suddenly I felt overwhelmed. "Drover, some parts of this conversation don't make any sense. I'm exhausted and I don't even know why."

"I'll be derned. Maybe we ought to scratch. It's easy and we're good at it."

I ran this information through Data Control. "You know, that's an interesting idea. It's good for a dog to do the things he's good at."

"Yeah, and good + good = gooder."

"Great point." I whopped him on the back. "Let's get after it. The last one to start scratching is a rotten egg."

And with that, we both sat down on our respective hinies and began hacking away at our ears. Within seconds, the air was filled with loose dog hairs, and a warm pleasant feeling swept over me. I never figured out how we'd gotten on the subject of pirates, but the important thing is that Drover and I had a great session of scratching.

Life was good again. I felt like a new dog, ready to go back to work, solving cases and protecting the ranch.

Does any of that make sense? Maybe not, but when you live with Drover twenty-four hours a day, you have to lower your expectations.

Alfred and I
Help Slim

I left Drover (he continued scratching) and drifted back to the area where the men were working on their little projects. Loper was still battling the wiper blade and Slim was watching. "Loper, you probably don't want to hear this."

"Then don't say it."

"But I'll say it anyway. It looks ignorant when a man changes out his wiper blades in the middle of a drought."

"That's the best time to do it, before it starts raining."

"By the time it rains, the rubber on the new blades will be rotten, and you'll have to do it all over again."

"If it rains, I won't care. I'd love to change

wiper blades in the rain."

"So would I, but it's looking like it ain't ever going to rain again."

"It'll rain, it always has, and every day we're getting closer to it." Loper got the wiper blade snapped into place and walked over to Slim. "Are you going to pack those wheel bearings or yap all day?"

"I'm getting it done, just needed a little break. It's hot. Lookie yonder." He pointed toward the big Dr. Pepper thermometer on the front of the machine shed. It showed 95 degrees. "And the radio says it's supposed to go to 107 tomorrow."

"So the heat is bothering you?"

"Well, I'm not one to complain, but yes, it's kind of hot out here."

Loper smiled. "I can fix that."

He strolled into the barn, came out with a flat-blade screwdriver, and removed the two screws that were holding the thermometer to the side of the barn. He pitched it onto the seat of his pickup and gave Slim a fanged smile. "There, that ought to help. If you'll quit looking at the thermometer, you won't have any reason to feel sorry for yourself."

"Loper, that's childish."

"Look, buddy, our daddies hauled hay and

built fence in this kind of heat. You know how they did it? They didn't listen to the weather report or look at the thermometer. They went to work. Try it."

Slim shook his head and grinned. "Loper, you're a piece of work. By the way, happy birthday. What are you, ninety-five?"

"Thanks. You can leave my gifts at the house. I'm going to look at the pastures up north. If they look as bad as I think, we might have to start selling cows, and we'll need that stock trailer to haul horses. If you can work it into your schedule to grease the wheel bearings, that would be nice."

Loper climbed into his pickup and drove off. Slim grumbled under his breath and went back to work. I sat down in the shade and did some Anti-Flea work on my left ear. Moments later, who or whom do you suppose arrived on the scene? Little Alfred.

He had wandered up to the machine shed to see what was causing all the noise (the air wrench). By that time, Slim had pulled both tires off the right side of the stock trailer, had removed the hubs and pulled the bearings off the axles, and now he was "packing the bearings."

Do you know what that means? Neither did I, but I soon found out. He was packing the bearings with grease, thick gooey stuff that came in a big can. Wheel bearings last longer when they've got grease, don't you see. If you don't give 'em grease, they get hot and...I don't know, burn up or fall off or something like that.

Trailer bearings have to be packed with grease twice a year, is the point, and Slim had drawn the job. There he sat on a five-gallon bucket, pushing grease into the rollers of the wheel bearing. Sweat dripped off the end of his nose and he had smudges of grease on his shirt, both cheeks, and the tip of his chin.

Alfred said, "Hi Swim, whatcha doing?"

"I'm playing in the grease and making a mess. That's what the boss told me to do."

"Maybe I can help."

Slim's eyes came up, and he looked...well, crabby. "I've got tools and parts scattered over half an acre. Don't mess with my stuff."

Alfred stood around for a while, then he went to work. While Slim was busy, he pulled several wrenches from the tool box and used them to dig a hole in the ground. Then he caught a grasshopper and pushed him into the can of grease, and walked off with a three-quarter-inch socket.

After a while, we heard Slim's voice. "Where's that box-end wrench?" He tore through the tool box, rattling tools. "I swear, sharing a set of tools with Loper is like working with a chimpanzee. In his whole life, the man has never put a tool back where it belongs."

He stormed into the machine shed, which produced more banging and clanging. Alfred drifted over to the trailer and picked up the wheel bearing. He looked at it for a while, then laid it on the fender of the trailer—not where he'd found it.

Uh oh.

When Slim came out of the machine shed, his teeth were clinched and his face had turned red. "How can I keep the machinery running on this ranch when the boss carries off all my tools?"

He flopped himself down on the bucket and glanced around. "Now, what did I do with that bearing? I set it down right there. I thought I did." He got up and went back into the machine shed. We heard clanging, banging, and muttering. He came out shaking his head. "What did I do with the dadgum bearing?"

He walked around the trailer, looking everywhere but on the fender. He shook his head in despair. "I'm losing my mind, and I didn't have much to start with."

Well, this seemed to be a time when a loyal

dog could make a contribution. I mean, I knew exactly where the bearing had gone, so I barked.

"You hush."

Fine. I could hush. By George, if they don't want help from their dogs, they can do things the hard way. What a grouch.

He sat down on the bucket and tried to remember what he'd been doing before he stopped doing what he'd been doing and had started doing something else. "Now where'd the socket go?" He picked up the can of grease and stared into it. "Who put the grasshopper in the...Alfred!"

The boy came over, looking as innocent as a lamb. Slim pointed to the grasshopper. "Is this some of your work?"

Alfred nodded. "He needed some gwease."

"He needed some grease. Did you steal my wrenches?"

The boy nodded. "I dug a hole."

"You dug a hole. Okay, here's the bonus question. Did you haul off my wheel bearing?" Alfred bobbed his head and pointed to the bearing.

Slim's lips moved but no words came out. He slapped his hands on his knees and pushed himself up to his full height. "An idle mind is the devil's workshop. Y'all are fired, both of you. Get out of here, scat! If you come around here again,

37

I'm going to haul you both to the dog pound."

I think that business about the dog pound might have been a joke, but he was on such a snort, I didn't want to test it, and neither did Alfred. As we walked away, the lad whispered, "I was just trying to help."

Yes, I understood. The harder you try to please some people, the more they don't appreciate your effort. On this outfit, no good deed goes unseated.

No good deed goes unpunished, let us say.

Anyway, Little Alfred and I had gotten fired, so we had to find something else to do. But what?

That's a problem on long, hot summer days. See, we lived twenty-five miles from town and there wasn't a whole lot going on.

We drifted over to a spot of shade on the west side of the water storage tank, and there we joined...guess who. Mister Half-Stepper. He was lying in the shade like the Great Sphinx, only he wasn't even close to being great. A sawed-off, stub-tailed little mutt, is what he was, but I had to admit that he had a talent for finding good shade.

"Move."

I pushed him out of the way and took his spot beside the storage tank, which always stayed cool in the summertime. Alfred flopped down beside me, hugged his knees with both arms, and looked out at the heat waves on the horizon. The minutes dragged by.

Then the boy cocked his head and grinned. "I know what we can do. Oh, this'll be fun!"

He leaped up and trotted down to the house.

I thought about leaping up and trotting beside him, but...hey, it was hot, and we're talking about succotashing heat. *Suffocating* heat, let us say. Succotash is some kind of food dish, right? It has nothing to do with heat unless you warm it up in the oven, but even then...never mind.

As I was saying, broiling heat makes a dog want to homestead a shady spot beside the water storage tank. Don't get me wrong, I had no desire to be a lazy bum like Drover, but there are times when...well, bumhood is kind of appealing, and I'll have to give the runt credit for one thing. He'd found the best piece of shade on the whole ranch, and I appreciated that he'd invited me to share it with him.

Okay, he didn't exactly invite me, and we didn't exactly share. I pulled rank and *took* the shady spot. Heh heh. That's one of the perks of being Head of Ranch Security, don't you see. We get first dibs on the shade. Naturally, he moaned and whined.

"You took my shade."

"All our lines are busy. Call back in an hour."

"I'm hot."

"Winter will be here before you know it."

"What if I get heat stroke?"

"I'll send flowers."

"I don't think you even care."

"You could be right."

"It's not fair."

"Right again. Hush."

Some dogs need more ignoring than others, and Drover requires constant ignoring. We call it

"Drover Deaf." I let him blabber all he wants. He feels better, complaining, and I feel better, ignoring everything he says.

I had drifted off into a great little snooze, when a sound reached my ears and brought me back to the world of worry, care, and responsibility. From somewhere in the distance, I heard the voice of a child, calling out, "Here, Pete! Here, doggies! Food!"

Huh?

CHAPTER FIVE

An Unscheduled Food Event

As you know, we dogs are very sensitive to any sound that might suggest Scrap Time: the slamming of the screen door at the house, the scrape of a fork over a plate, the squeak of the hinges on the yard gate, or any mention of "food." Any one of those sounds will grab our attention. It doesn't matter what we're doing at the moment. We head for the house to check things out.

Scrap Time brings meaning and purpose into a dog's life, don't you see, especially on a hot summer day. But don't forget that Alfred had said more than "food." He had also called Pete. In other words, there appeared to be some danger that he would GIVE OUR FOOD REWARD TO THE CAT!

I guess you know my position on that issue. Giving scraps to the cat is more than a waste of our precious natural resources. It's immoral and unpatriotic. It rewards our local cat for being a moocher and leads to corruption at the lowest levels of ranch society.

Sorry, I don't mean to rave, but this issue really gets me worked up. We're talking about greed and gluttony. It's a matter of principle, high principle, and when I heard Alfred calling the cat to our Food Event...well, someone needed to put a stop to this outrage, and to make sure that Sally May's little crook of a cat got no scraps.

None. That's our policy: zero scraps for the cat, and if we have to administer a thrashing and run him up a tree, so much the better.

I turned to Drover and was about to give the order to Launch All Dogs, when I noticed that... hmm, the little mutt had curled up in a ball and was taking a nap. He hadn't heard anything and...well, all at once it became clear that I should *let him sleep*.

He needed his rest, no kidding. I mean, he had a limp, right? Limping around all day uses up a lot of energy, and don't forget his allergies. Sneezing and sniffling will sure drag you down.

Yes, my assistant had worn himself out, and

43

seeing him in this state of deep fatigue touched me all the way to the bottom of my stomach...all the way to the bottom of my *heart*, let us say. The little guy needed the healing tonic that can only come from a period of peaceful sleep, so I, uh, crept away on tiptoes, so as not to disturb his scraps.

So as not to disturb his *slumber*.

Only then did I hit Full Flames on all engines and go streaking down to the scene of the crime, although no crime had been committed...yet. It was my job to see that it didn't happen.

Crime Prevention is what we call it, and I knew that if Drover had been awake and alert, he would have been cheering me on. That was one thing I had always appreciated about the little guy, his tireless support of our many Crime Prevention programs. No kidding.

I went streaking down the hill and arrived just as Little Alfred was coming out of the yard gate. It appeared that I had gotten there just in the nickering of time: *no cat*. I hit Air Brakes, slid to a stop, sat down on the ground, and went into a little program we call "I Might Perish If I Don't Get Some Scraps."

At the same time, I checked his hands to see if...well, I expected to see him carrying a fork and a plate. Fork + Plate = Scraps. I mean, that was the whole point of my being there, right? Scraps.

I saw no plate or fork. Instead, he was carrying some kind of large round plastic container. Rats. Nobody on this ranch had ever delivered scraps in a large round plastic container, and my spirits took a plunge into the dark pit of...something.

It's hard to describe the gloom that falls upon a dog when he finds himself facing a day with no scraps. And to make the day even gloomier, Drover arrived at that very moment, huffing and puffing.

I melted him with a glare. "What are you doing here? I thought you were asleep."

"Well, I was, but I heard the gate squeak. How come you didn't wake me up?"

"I thought you needed your rest. I did it for my own...I did it for your own good. You've been acting sickly."

"Yeah, by dose is stobbed ub, but I'm dever too sig for scrabs."

"Well, you wasted your time. There are no scraps."

"No scraps?" His face collapsed. "Gosh, what'll we do?"

"We'll think about all the scraps we didn't get.

For twenty-four hours, our lives will lose all meaning and purpose."

"Oh drat. I'm not sure I can stand it." A look of desolation came over his face. "My life didn't have much meaning to start with, and now this!"

"I know, but try to be brave. We'll just have to trudge on with…" Suddenly my nose shot upward and began pulling in air samples. Unless I was badly mistaken, my instruments were picking up the smell of something…sweet.

I did a wide scan with Snifforadar and zeroed in on that plastic thing in Alfred's hands. He had removed the lid, don't you see, and I noticed an interesting twinkle in his eyes. He said, "My mom baked a cake."

Oh, so that was it! His mom had baked a cake and she'd given him a piece, and now he was going to share it with his doggie friends. What a fine young man and what a great idea!

You know, we dogs don't get too many chances to enjoy cake because…well, our people are kind of stingy with their baked goods. Might as well be honest about it. They're generous with all the stuff they don't want, the corn cobs and baked potato hulls, but seldom do we ever see a slice of cake.

So what we had here was a major event in the

history of our ranch, a boy and his dogs sharing a slice of cake. The water works in my mouth began pumping and my tail flogged the ground. I inched closer and directed my nose toward...

He pushed me away. "No no, Hankie. We're all going to share one little piece, but you have to be nice and wait your turn."

Share? Be nice? Bummer. Oh well, if being polite was the price for a bite of cake, so be it, but could we hurry up? There's a limit on how long we can do Nice Doggie in front of a piece of...

I looked closer and, holy smokes, that wasn't just a *slice* of cake. He'd brought the WHOLE THING, a beautiful angel-food cake with thick, creamy icing!

"It's my dad's birthday cake."

I stared at him. WHAT? That was his dad's birthday cake...and he had smuggled it out of the house?

I backed away. What we had here was an explosion waiting to happen. Boredom had pushed this kid beyond the reach of common sense. Just think about it. Number One, he would get caught. He always got caught, because his mother had Radar For Naughty Behavior. She saw everything.

Number Two, when she figured out what was

going on, any member of our ranch community who had crumbs or icing on his mouth would be… wow, I didn't even want to think about it.

Which brings us to Point Three: you should never give a dog more temptation than he can handle. I was reminded of this when I noticed Drover's sudden transformation. The little mutt was showing all the signs of Cake Convulsions: wild eyes, dripping chops, tongue hanging out the left side of his mouth, the whole nine yards of CC.

In a crazy voice, he said, "He brought a whole cake!"

I moved into position to block his view of the cake. "Get hold of yourself, son. We've been lured into a very dangerous situation and the Security Division is going to walk away from it."

"Yeah, but…"

"There's nothing for us here but trouble"

"There's an angel-food cake, and I love cake!"

"I know you love cake and so do I, but there are times when we must use our training and discipline to avoid a catastrophe. Do an about-face. We're going to march back to the office."

He pointed a paw and stammered, "C-c-c-c-cat!"

"Exactly. Cat-as-tro-phe. It's a four-cylinder word that means disaster, and it's something we

don't need. Let's go."

"No, it's the cat!"

Huh?

I whirled around and saw Trouble rubbing its way down the yard fence, its insolent little tail sticking straight up in the air. Can you guess who it was? Mister Kitty Moocher, and he had come to mooch a piece of our cake.

That would never happen, not as long as I was running the Security Division, not as long as I still had a breath of body left in my air. By George, if anyone on this ranch mooched some cake, it would be a dog, not a scheming little cat... only we dogs weren't going to get involved in it, so neither would the cat.

The entire world went red at that moment, and I turned to face the approach of the cat. I had no idea that events were fixing to sweep us all away like a raging river.

You'll never guess what happened, so you'd better keep reading. I guarantee that you'll be shocked.

CHAPTER SIX

There Are No Teensie Weensie Temptations

As the cat approached, my lips curled into a snarl and I delivered a Warning Bark. "That's far enough, Kitty. This is a private meeting and you're not invited."

Did he take the hint? Of course not. Cats don't take hints, and here he came, slithering down the fence. After he had rubbed all the rust off the hog wire, he came to the open gate. There, he ran out of something upon which to rub on which.

At that point, he batted his eyes, pranced through the gate, cranked up his purring machine, and flashed that annoying little smirk that drives me nuts.

"Well, well! It's Hankie the Wonderdog."

Things began happening in the control room of my mind. Lights flashed and gongs gonged and buzzers buzzed. A voice came over the radio. "The target has closed to three yards. Speed five knots. Bearing oh-two-zero-five. Flood tubes one and three. Arm the weapons. We have a solution light. Stand by to launch!"

I rose to my feet and swung the bow into the wow...into the wind, let us say. My head and neck formed a deadly straight line, aimed directly at the target. The hair rose on the back of my neck. I went to Lift-up on the Tooth Shields and heard a rumble deep in my throat. We were ready to launch.

But then...a voice. "Hankie!"

Huh?

The boy was scowling at me. "Don't be mean to the cat."

Me? Hey, I hadn't even touched the little snot. Okay, something about my body language might have, uh, revealed my thoughts, but strictly speaking, I hadn't done anything.

Alfred shook a finger at me. "We're gonna have ourselves a picnic and eat some cake, but y'all have to be nice."

I moved closer to the boy and used my eyes, ears, and tail to deliver an urgent message.

"Alfred, listen to a friend. This is a BAD idea. It was a bad idea even before the cat showed up. Take the cake back to the house. Cancel the picnic."

Did he receive the message? It was hard to tell. He held up some kind of silver tool. Okay, it was a cake knife. "We'll share one teensie weensie, little bitty piece, that's all. My dad won't care."

His dad might not care, but his mom would blow a fuse. I knew her and I could guarantee it. Furthermore...this next part was hard to express, but I had to try. I moved closer.

"Alfred, son, there are things you don't understand. In my world, there's no such thing as a Teensie Weensie Temptation. Temptation comes in one size: HUGE. You need to trust me on this."

I searched his face and saw that he wasn't getting it. How could he NOT get it? All he had to do was look at Drover, who was still going through convulsions. We're talking about burning eyes, dripping tongue, frothy mouth, the whole nine yards of frenzied cake desire.

The cat too. By that time, the little pest had caught the scent of the cake and a weird, wild look had come into his eyes. So far, I had managed to keep a tight rein on my own symptoms, but... let's be honest here. I was getting worried about this.

"Drover, quick, let's get out of here."

"Yeah, but..."

"Don't argue with me. Back to the barracks. Move!"

I gave the runt a hard shove and we marched away from this disaster-in-the-making. Whew! I knew that Little Alfred was fixing to get himself into a boat-load of trouble, but at least I wouldn't be...

Then it happened. When the greedy little cat saw that Law Enforcement was pulling away from the scene, he seized his opportunity to rob the bank. He climbed up Alfred's pant leg and dived right into the middle of the cake.

"Pete, no!"

Too late. I whirled around, just in time to see the tragedy unfolding. The plastic container slipped out of Alfred's grasp and fell. The cake rolled out onto the ground and the thieving little cat jumped right in the middle of it, while the boy watched with a look of horror on his face.

See? When they don't listen to their dogs, this is what happens.

Okay, that did it. Code Three. I hit Sirens and

Lights and rushed back to the scene. Kitty didn't want to leave the cake, but I was able to root him out and send him back to the iris patch.

"There, you little crook, and let that be a lesson to you!"

I whirled around and started back to the cake, and that's when I saw something that almost broke my heart. One of my own men, my assistant Head of Ranch Security, had taken the cat's place. Drover was in the middle of the cake. Alfred was trying to pull him off, but the little dunce had lost what was left of his mind, and was gobbling like a maniac.

I zoomed back to the scene. "Okay, that's enough! Drover, hands up and back away, move it!"

He lifted his head and stared at me. He had an icing mustache and looked ridiculous. "Yeah, but..."

"I'm so ashamed of you, I don't know what to say."

"Yeah, but..."

"You've broken discipline and yielded to temptation. You're acting just like a common alley cat!"

"Yeah, but..."

"Go to your room immediately. I'll deal with you later."

He left, hanging his head and sniffling, and I turned my full attention to Little Alfred. He flopped down beside the ruins of his daddy's birthday cake and buried his face in his hands. The kid was on the virgil of tears and needed some help. I stepped forward and gave him licks on the face.

He uncovered his eyes and gave me a pleading look. "Hankie, they ruined my dad's cake. What am I going to do? If my mom finds out..." He started crying.

You know, a lot of dogs would have walked away and left the kid to face the music all by himself. I mean, I had tried to warn him and he hadn't listened. But you know how I am about these kids. My slurp goes out to them.

My heart, that is.

I licked the tears off his cheeks and beamed him a message that said, "Hush now, don't cry. I'll clean up the mess and dispose of the evidence. Maybe your mother will think...I don't know, maybe she'll think the cake flew away or something."

He smiled, and fellers, let me tell you, it was as though the sun had peeked out from behind a big black cloud. In my line of work, there's nothing that brings us more satisfaction than helping a little friend when he's gotten himself into a hopeless mess.

But now I had to get to work.

Most dogs wouldn't attempt to eat a whole cake at one sitting. I mean, that was a BIG cake. I wasn't sure I could handle the job, but I had to give it my best shot.

I stuck my face into the cake and went to work. We're talking about a high-powered vacuum sweeper or one of those big machines that clears deep snow off a highway, a four-legged high-tech device that had been designed for this very project—cleaning up crime scenes and protecting little children from...

"ALFRED LEROY, WHAT ON EARTH ARE YOU DOING!"

Huh?

I'd heard a voice in the distance, a loud piercing voice, but it was calling "Alfred Leroy," and, well, that wasn't me, so I continued to sweep and mop the scene. Maybe the person who belonged to the voice would go away. That happens sometimes, right?

Gobble, gulp, smack.

In a quiet sector of my mind, I heard the squeak of the gate and the sound of footsteps approaching. Or maybe it was just my imagination.

That happens sometimes, right? I ignored it and tried to concentrate on my work.

Then I heard another voice. It said, and this is a direct quote, it said, "Hankie, stop! My mom's coming!"

HUH?

Somehow the word "mom" penetrated the outer layers of steel that encased the Control Room of My Mind. It was a tiny word, only three letters, but somehow it, uh, resonated. I stopped gobbling, lifted my head, and...

Yipes.

I blinked my eyes and ran Damage Assessment. Bad. Real bad.

There she stood, looming over me like one of those giant redwood trees, two hundred feet tall, only trees don't have faces. This one had a face and it froze my gizzard.

Well, a dog can't expect to live forever and I'd had a pretty good life. My last wish was that they would carve a message on my tombstone that would sum up my whole career: "Anything for the kids."

In the poisonous silence, I went to Slow Mournful taps on the tail section, and waited for the hammer to fall. I mean, I knew something awful was coming. I could see thoughts flashing across her face and, well, they weren't encouraging. Dangerous.

I waited for an explosion, but nobody said a word. It was creepy. I could hear Sally May's rapid breathing and Alfred's sniffles. Then the dam broke. The boy started bawling, rushed to his mother, and hugged her legs, and she burst out crying and put an arm around him, and they both sank to the ground and bawled and hugged.

Wow. I didn't know whether to stick around or run for my life.

Through her sobs, Sally May moaned, "It took me two hours to make that cake!" I thought about rushing over to give her some comfort, but then she wailed, "I don't know how long it takes to murder a dog."

Yipes. I cancelled that idea.

Alfred gave his head a hard shake. "No, Mom, it wasn't his fault. He was just trying to help."

That produced a chilling cackle. "Of course! I didn't think of that. He was trying to help!"

"Honest, Mom. It was my fault, all my fault! It was so dumb...and now you're going to hate me!"

Sally May stopped crying, wiped her eyes, and looked into his face. "Honey, don't ever say that. Don't ever *think* that. Never, never! You made a bad decision and we both feel bad about it, but..." She caught her breath and pushed a sprig of hair away from her face. "It was only a cake."

"I'm sorry, Mom. I ruined my dad's birthday."

She pulled him into her embrace. "Honey, he doesn't care about birthdays anyway, and maybe we can make him another cake. What do you think? Would you help me?"

Alfred cried on her shoulder and nodded his little head.

This was a very touching scene, and exactly the wrong time for someone to interrupt the mood with an uncouth belching sound, but sometimes, when you eat too fast, it happens. It just snuck out and I sure didn't mean any disrespect.

BORP.

Sally May flinched and her gaze came at me like a spear, and for a moment of heartbeats, I didn't know what might come next. Would she leap to her feet and try to wring my neck?

To be honest, I wouldn't have been surprised. But to my great relief, a smile tugged at the corners of her mouth. "I guess you liked my cake."

Oh yes, delicious. Awesome cake, loved the icing, and as a matter of fact...sniff, sniff...now that the storm had passed, I figured it wouldn't hurt...

"Hank, I think you'd better leave. Now. Goodbye. Scat!"

Yes ma'am, exactly my thoughts. A guy never wants to push his luck. I did an about-face and hurried away. Behind me, I heard her voice. "And thanks for all your help."

Glad to do it.

Borp.

A Huge Moral
Victory Over the Cat

I wasn't sure whether Sally May was being sincere or making a joke, but she wasn't chasing me with a broom, so you'd have to say it turned out pretty well. Boy, I had dodged an artillery shell on that deal.

I hurried away, then slowed my steps. And stopped. The thought had just occurred to me... what was she going to do with the, uh, ruins of the cake? Drover and the cat had pretty muchly wrecked it beyond repair. And, okay, I had done a little damage to it myself, but the point is that the cake was in no condition to be used to celebrate anyone's birthday.

I sat down and watched. Sally May and Alfred had their cry. They hugged and made up, and soon they were laughing. Sally May suggested that they pull weeds in what was left of the garden. (The funny thing about this drought was that the deer and rabbits were eating the vegetables and leaving all the weeds).

They walked away from the cake and started south, toward the garden. My tongue swept across my lips and I could hear my tail slapping the ground. But then...rats...Sally May went back, scooped up the cake into the plastic container, and dumped it into the trash barrel.

Okay, we would have to refigure this deal. As soon as she started pulling weeds...

"Hank, don't you dare tip over the garbage barrel and try to eat that cake!"

Huh?

Yes ma'am. I would never...you see what I mean about Sally May? No dog is safe around her. Privacy? Forget it. She sees into every corner of a dog's mind. Phooey.

I whirled around and began marching toward the machine shed. If you recall, I had sent Drover to his room and we needed to get started on his court martial. The charge this time would be Gluttony and Shameless Destruction of a Cake. I had gone about a dozen steps when I heard another voice behind me, and this one belonged to the cat.

"Oh, Hankie? Don't worry about the cake. I'll take care of it."

I froze. Our missile batteries swung around and sonar detected a potential target lurking in the iris patch. I tossed a glance to the south. Sally May was busy in the garden and nobody was watching the yard.

Would we have time to deliver a quick strike on the iris patch?

Data Control chewed on the numbers and flashed a message across the screen of my mind: "Full-scale bombardment too risky. Try diplomacy."

With great effort, I forced a pleasant expression upon my face and made a casual stroll over to the yard fence. "Hi, Pete. You said something about the cake?"

"Um hmm. I can jump into the trash barrel without tipping it over. It's something cats can do."

A snarl quivered at my lips. "How interesting. I hadn't thought of that. So you're saying…"

"I'll finish cleaning up the cake. But, well, I wanted to be sure that was all right. I'd hate it if you felt…bitter."

The way he spoke that word made it sting like a wasp, but I couldn't allow myself to show it.

"Me? Bitter? Ha ha. Not at all, Pete. Hey, come over here and we'll talk."

"Talk about what, Hankie?"

"Oh, you know, keeping the ranch neat and tidy. That's a big deal and we all need to do our part."

I didn't expect the little dummy to fall for this, but he did. See, cats are pretty shrewd when it comes to cheap tricks, but they have one huge, glaring weakness: over-confidence. I don't want to reveal too many of our secrets, but maybe it won't hurt to whisper this.

All our diplomatic efforts are calculated to take advantage of this flaw in cats.

We toss 'em a bone, see, and let 'em win the Little Game, while we set 'em up for the Big Game.

Heh heh. Is that wicked or what? The mind of a dog is an awesome thing.

Here he came, slithering out of his hideout in the iris patch, rubbing his way down the fence, purring, smirking, and holding his arrogant little tail straight up in the air.

As I watched this shameless display, I felt various parts of my body going off in twitches and quivers, mainly the eyes, ears, and lips. I had to disable the Main Circuit to prevent a blowout that would have exposed the true purpose of my so-called "diplomatic effort".

Suddenly he was there, two feet in front of my nose, with nothing but a hog wire fence between us.

Your ordinary ranch mutts know nothing about this level of self-restraint. They live from moment to moment and are slaves to their emotions. They go blundering into every situation without a plan.

But those of us who claw our way to the top and become Heads of Ranch Security mutts muster the dipple of self-restraint. Let me rephrase that. We must *master* the *discipline* of self-restraint.

And I hate it. Self-restraint stinks, especially when you've got a sniveling cat sitting two feet in front of you. But for those of us who live at the top of the mountain, restraint is a tool we use to accomplish a broader purpose. I had plans for Kitty.

He was grinning and purring and licking the icing off his paw. "Well, here I am, Hankie. But are you sure you don't mind if I..." He flashed a grin, "...clean up the cake?"

I was trembling inside. "Not a problem, Pete. I mean, there's no sense in letting good cake go to waste. But you know, it would be easier to talk if you came a little closer."

"It would be easier, wouldn't it?"

"Oh yes, more comfortable and relaxed."

"I agree."

"Good. Hop over the fence."

He gazed up at the clouds. "If you don't mind, Hankie, I think I'll stay here in the yard. It's such a nice yard."

"It's a great yard."

"So nice and green, while the rest of the ranch is brown with drought." He flicked the end of his tail back and forth. "Does it bother you that Sally May doesn't allow dogs in her yard?"

"Ha ha. Not at all, Pete. Oh, maybe a little bit. Sometimes. Okay, it rips me up one side and down the other, but let's don't get started on that."

"I agree. And let's don't say a word about..." He sputtered a laugh, "...how you got caught eating the cake. It was so sad!"

"You bet it was, since you're the little sneak who knocked it out of Alfred's hands."

"I know. It just doesn't seem fair." He moved closer to the fence, only twelve inches away from our missile batteries. "You got the blame and when Sally May goes back to the house, I'll finish the cake." He snickered and shook his head. "It's just amazing. You keep walking into the propeller. How does that happen?"

Steam was hissing out of my ears. "Ha ha. Great question, Pete. Come a little closer and I'll whisper the answer."

His eyes lit up. "Will you? Oh goodie!"

He moved right against the fence, and I couldn't hold myself back any longer. Self-restraint went up in smoke. I launched myself against the fence and gave the cat one of my Train Horn Barks, right in the face.

BWONK!

I was a little surprised when he, well, delivered a left jab to my nose. Bam! Okay, if that's the way he wanted it...

BWONK!

Bam, bam, pop!

Three jabs in a row. "That was a lucky punch, Kitty."

"Which one? I threw so many, my arm's getting numb."

"Oh yeah? I'll show you numb!"

I lunged against the fence and blasted him with another bark, this time Ocean Liner.

BWONK!

Bam, bam, pop!

Okay, I had figured out his game plan. The little sneak thought he could take my nose apart with his jabs, but I had news for him. I revved up all engines and flung myself against the fence, and this time, I had every intention of taking it OUT, and we're talking about posts, wire, staples, the gate, every bit of it.

Bam, bam, pop!

Let's skip the rest of this. Never mind. Nothing happened.

It's been hot, hasn't it? They say it's one of the hottest summers in years, and also terribly dry. Our grass looks pathetic and Loper has been talking about...

Look, it doesn't take any skill or brains to hide behind a hog wire fence and shoot out jabs. Anyone could do it. If you want to be a fighter, come out and fight. If you want to be a little chicken, stay inside the yard and...phooey.

He makes me sick, and one of these days...you know, he was so fat and out of shape, I wore him out. He was on the ropes, ready to go down. You know what saved him?

Sally May heard my Train Horns and yelled, "Hank, leave the cat alone!"

One more minute and he would have been hamburger. I whirled around and marched away.

Behind me, I heard him deliver one last cheap shot. "Don't walk into any propellers, Hankie!"

See what I mean? Nobody does the cheap shot better than a cat.

I needed to do a little work on blocking those jabs, but in the Larger Scheme of Things, I had won a huge moral victory. Kitty would devour the rest of the cake, but he would have to eat it, all alone, in a dark, lonely trash barrel—because HE HAD NO FRIENDS.

Give me a choice between cake and friends, and I'll...phooey.

Fire!

Anyway, it was time for me to take care of my business with Drover: place him under arrest and get his court martial out of the way. I had sent him to his room, but I knew where to look for him: in his Secret Sanctuary, the machine shed, the place where he flees to escape all the burdens of normal life.

I stuck my nose through the crack in the double doors. "Drover?" Nothing, not a sound. "Drover, I know you're in here. Hello?" Not a sound. "Drover, we need to talk."

At last, I heard his faint reply. "Talk about what?"

"Your career. We need to discuss that little promotion."

"No fooling? You're not mad?"

"Mad? Me? Ha ha. Report to the front, and please hurry. I've got a busy schedule today."

I waited for what seemed hours, but at last, he came lollygagging out of the gloom. He was wearing a silly grin. "Boy, old Pete sure did a number on your nose."

"What makes you think Pete did anything to my nose?"

"Well, I watched."

"Oh, so you watched? That must have been fun."

"Yeah, hee hee, I couldn't believe you kept going back for more of his home cooking."

"Home cooking? That's a clever way of putting it. Sit down, make yourself comfortable." He flopped his bohunkus on the cement and I began pacing a circle around him. "Tell this court exactly what you felt as you watched your commanding officer endure a blizzard of jabs from the stupid cat."

"Well, it was pretty funny."

"Did you laugh?"

"Oh yeah, like crazy. I couldn't help it."

"In other words, you enjoyed watching your commanding officer suffer this humiliating experience? Is that what you're telling this

court?"

"Well…"

"If you could express the entertainment factor in pounds, how many pounds of laughter did you receive?"

He rolled his eyes around. "Let's see…ten or twelve."

"Then it's settled. For every pound of pleasure you got out of that shameful fiasco, *you will spend an hour with your nose in the corner.*"

"Yeah, but…"

"This court is adjourned. Prisoner will be removed to the brig, where he will serve twelve hours of Nose Time." I shot out a paw toward the nearest corner. "Move."

"Yeah, but I didn't do anything."

"You should have thought of that sooner. Next time, maybe you'll do something, and we'll court-martial you for that too."

I marched the prisoner to the southeast corner of the machine shed. "There. Put your nose in the corner, and think about what a lousy friend you've turned out to be."

"Twelve whole minutes?"

"That was the verdict of the court, twelve minutes in solitary confinement, and I don't want to hear any grumbling."

I hated to be so severe with the runt, but if the officers don't take the time to discipline the men, how will they learn anything?

The bad part of this deal was that I didn't dare leave him alone in his cell. I knew he would cheat. Don't forget: he had a cozy relationship with the local cat, so I had every reason to suppose that he would cheat any time the opportunity presented itself.

Ho hum. Boy, you talk about time crawling! After five minutes, I was about to go nuts. I rose to my feet and paced over to his cell. "Drover, the Review Board has been looking at your case. We're considering an early release. All we require is that you swear a Solomon Oath."

"Oh goodie, I can handle that."

"Raise your right paw and repeat..." My nose was picking up an odor. "I smell smoke."

"I smell smoke."

"Smoke is a bad thing to smell in a drought."

"Smell is a bad thing to smoke in a joke."

"Stop repeating what I say."

"Stop repeating what I..."

"Drover, snap out of it! Don't you get it? Smoke in the air means we're downwind from a prairie fire!"

His eyes grew as wide as two fried eggs. "Fire!

Oh my gosh, I think I'll faint."

And before my very eyes, that's what he did, went over like a bicycle, just as a vehicle pulled into the gravel drive in front of the machine shed. I left Drover where he lay and rushed outside.

Loper jumped out of the pickup and yelled, "There's a fire on Parnell's! Saddle the horses, we've got to move the cows out of this pasture!"

On an ordinary day, Slim didn't move at dazzling speed, but this woke him up. He leaped to his feet and gazed off to the south, where a big column of angry white smoke was rising in the air.

"Good honk!"

"Looks like the wind's taking it east of the house, but it's going to burn the home pasture. I'll call the fire department. Saddle two horses."

Loper trotted down to the house and—this will really surprise you—Slim *ran* down the hill to the saddle shed. I'm not kidding, he ran. I won't say that he was poetry in motion, but by George, he was pickin' 'em up and layin' 'em down.

Me? I did what any normal American dog would have done. I dashed back and forth in front of the machine shed and barked for five solid minutes, huge barks that kept the blaze away from headquarters.

Boy, what a relief! I mean, getting your pastures burned is bad enough, but at least the house and barns appeared to be safe. It makes you wonder what happens to ranches that don't have dogs, and I guess the answer is…they burn to the ground.

Well, things started happening fast. Loper made his phone call, ran out of the house, and drove his pickup down to the corrals. I headed that way myself. I knew they would need my help on this deal. As I raced past the chicken house, I saw J.T. Cluck herding twenty-seven hens to safety.

He squawked, "Y'all get inside, hurry! The British are coming!" As I rushed past, he yelled, "What did I tell you, pooch?"

"Good call, J.T."

What a dunce.

Minutes later, Loper and Slim were a-horseback, and they left the corrals in a high lope. I fell into position behind them and away we went. As we passed the house, Sally May came out into the yard and shouted, "Loper, don't take any chances, please!"

And he yelled back, "Hon, the banker owns forty percent of those cows. We've got to save them!"

From the house, the guys galloped east until they found cows that had come down to the creek for water and were lying around in the shade. Slim rode to the east side of the bunch, Loper stayed on the west, and I took the territory between them. By this time, we were working in a thick cloud of smoke, and that was a bad sign. It meant that we were directly in the path of the fire, and the wind was driving it toward us.

We pushed fifty cows and fifty calves through the smoke and toward the north. After a bit, we came to the county road and drove them across. There, I paused to catch my breath and threw a glance back to the south.

Good grief, the fire had reached the creek, and through the smoke, I could see huge cottonwood trees glowing like torches! A big cedar tree on the north side of the creek exploded in a burst of flames. The fire had jumped the creek and was headed our way!

We sure needed to hurry up, but the cows were hot and full of water, and they didn't want to move. I mean, how dumb is a cow that wants to lie down in the shade and become roast beef? That's how dumb they were, multiplied by fifty.

On a normal cattle drive, the cowboys move at

a slow pace and don't yell, and any cowboy who does is considered an "owl-headed rookie," to use the proper terminology. But this time it was different and all the rules of Cow-Handling Etiquette went out the window.

The cowboys yelled, waved their arms like crazy people, and used their lariat ropes as whips. Me? I barked, and we're talking about barks without pity and barks of great urgency.

Those cows didn't want to get out of a walk, but that was too bad for them. By George, forty percent of every one of those dummies belonged to the banker and...you know, I wasn't sure exactly what that meant, but Loper had said it with conviction, so it must have been important.

On and on we pushed through choking smoke until, at last, we came to a wire gate in the northeast corner of the home pasture. Slim dived out of the saddle, opened the gate, and threw it back, leaped into the saddle, and we pushed the herd through the gate and into the middle pasture.

Only then did I realize that we had come out of the smoke cloud. Slim and Loper gazed off in the east, where the fire was on a course that would destroy the grass on the east side of ranch. Now and then, through the smoke, we caught glimpses of fire trucks and heavy equipment, waging a battle to stop the beast.

Slim removed his hat and wiped the sweat off his face with the sleeve of his shirt. "Bad way to celebrate your birthday."

"Yeah, and the dog ate my cake."

"Well, look at the bright side. You didn't get barbecued, and we didn't lose any of the banker's cows."

Loper stared into the distance. "But we're going to lose at least half of our winter pasture, and look." He pointed toward the hay field. Through a gap in the smoke, we saw two big stacks of alfalfa hay going up in flames. "There goes the hay."

We dogs know our people pretty well, and when something's not right, we can see it on their faces. What I saw on Loper's face was...gloom.

CHAPTER NINE

Gloom Falls Over the Ranch

We started back to headquarters in a sad little procession. At the county road, we met a crew of volunteer fire fighters, three men in fire-fighting suits, riding in a big army surplus six-by-six truck. Loper flagged them down and asked how things were going.

The driver, a rancher from Lipscomb County, said, "We've got five motor graders cutting fire guards and I think they've got it stopped, if the wind doesn't change directions. But it got you pretty bad. From here on east, there isn't much left."

"That's what I figured. Anything we can do to help?"

"No, we'll sit on it for a few hours and let it

run its course. That's about all you can do. I'm sorry, Loper. A man doesn't need this in the middle of a drought."

Loper nodded. "Thanks for your help. We sure appreciate it."

We rode in silence all the way to the corrals—actually, the guys rode, I walked. Back at the pens, they pulled their saddles and bridles, and carried them into the saddle shed.

Loper leaned against the fence and stared at the ground. "We can't feed our way out of this drought and it would take a four-inch rain to bring this grass back to life." He took a deep breath of air and let it out slowly. "We're whipped. We're going to have to ship the cows."

Slim's eyes popped open. "All of them? Loper, if you take 'em to the sale barn, you'll be selling on a down-market."

"I know."

"When we get a rain and need to restock, cows'll be higher than a cat's back."

"I know."

"You can't sell cows for eight hundred bucks and buy 'em back for two thousand. The math don't work out."

"I know."

"Good honk, we'll be..."

Loper nodded.

A long silence followed, as each man was lost in his own thoughts. Then Slim said, "Should I start looking for another job?" Loper said nothing. "Loper?"

"We'll start gathering the north pastures day-after tomorrow and drive everything down to headquarters. I'll call Cesar and line up trucks."

"We'll need some cowboys."

Loper gave his head a shake. "I don't want anyone else around. This is like a funeral. Just you and me horseback...and Alfred. He can ride the pony. Sally May can call the cattle with the pickup." His eyes came up. "What about Viola? Doesn't she ride?"

"Oh yeah, she makes a hand."

"I don't mind having her around. Give her a call."

Slim gazed up at the sky for a long time—the pale blue, cloudless drought sky. "When I landed on this outfit, I was on my way to find a job in Montana. Maybe I'll get my chance after all."

Loper's eyes seemed empty. "I've never seen it this bad. I never thought I would see it this bad."

Boy, you talk about a bad ending to a bad day! All at once, our lives had been turned upside-down. The drought had stuck a dagger into the heart of our ranching operation, and the fire had finished the job. Loper was going to ship all the cattle. Slim was out of a job and would have to move.

Loper went to the house, and fellers, he looked like a man whose spirit had been smashed: empty eyes, head down, arms hanging at his sides. Standing in the yard, he gave the news to Sally May and she cried. Alfred tried to put on a brave face, but his lip was trembling. He didn't understand everything that was going on, but he'd never seen such a look of defeat in his daddy's eyes. And I guess he was feeling pretty blue about that deal with the cake too.

There was only one bright spot in this otherwise gloomy scene. Sally May's rotten little cat came creeping out of the iris patch and began rubbing on her ankles. When she turned to go inside the house, she stepped on his tail—and, fellers, she really nailed him.

"Reeeeeer!"

It didn't change anything, but, by George, if your world is falling apart, you might as well march into the Unknown with the sounds of an unhappy cat in your ears.

Drover and I hung around the corrals while Slim tended to the horses, put out feed, and finished his work on the stock trailer, then we hopped into his pickup and went down to his shack for the night. I had a feeling that he would appreciate having a couple of loyal dogs close by.

I mean, the guy was fixing to lose his job. That's a heavy load to be carrying around.

On the two-mile drive to his place, we drove past blackened pastures and trees that had been scorched, and the air was heavy with the smell of burned grass. Slim didn't say much, but Drover seemed to have gone over the edge. We're talking about hysterical.

"If Slim moves away, where'll we sleep on cold winter nights?"

"Drover, I don't know."

"We'll freeze!"

"We won't freeze."

"He won't be around to sing us corny songs or share his canned mackerel sandwiches." His eyes had grown wild. "Oh my gosh! What if times get so bad, Loper and Sally May have to eat their dogs?"

"They would never eat their dogs."

"If they sell all the cattle, they won't have any beef."

"Okay, have it your way. One of these days, we'll be a pot of soup."

"Help! I'm too young to be a pot of soup! And this leg's killing me!"

Oh brother. The little goof spun around in circles and dived into Slim's lap. There, he went into hiding with both paws covering his eyes. Slim seemed surprised and gave me a puzzled look. "What's wrong with Stub Tail? He's shaking all over."

Well, he didn't want to be a pot of soup. And he was a weird little hypocardiac. If he'd been back at headquarters, he would have dashed to the machine shed to hide from Life's unanswered questions, but in the cab of the pickup, his only place of refuge was a cowboy's lap.

Pot of soup. Oh brother.

Slim scratched the little mutt behind the ears. "I guess everybody's feeling low-down, even the dogs." He turned to me with a sad-sweet smile. "You might as well come over and join us."

No kidding? Hey, that sounded good to me. Actually, I didn't think that Loper and Sally May would eat their dogs, but I was feeling kind of uneasy about things, too, so I piled into his lap, alongside Drover. It was a little crowded, all three of us stacked into a small space under the steering wheel, but we were all together and it felt good.

Slim even nuzzled me with his chin, and I gave him a lick on the cheek. He didn't seem to mind, and I think he might have enjoyed it.

It was a precious moment, a cowboy and his dogs, driving the pickup home at the end of the day. And we were all thinking the same thought…that our time together was…well, coming to an end.

Yes, it was a golden moment, right up to the second when…you won't believe this…right up to the second when Mister Squeakbox....oh brother!

Slim felt something warm and wet spreading across his lap. His eyes popped wide open, he hit the brakes, and tossed both of us to the other side of the cab.

"Knotheads! That's what I get for being nice. Y'all have no more manners than a couple of hogs."

We made the rest of the trip in stony silence. Slim was really hacked about the wet spot on the front of his jeans, and I mean, a big wet spot. I was so mad at Drover, I couldn't speak. When we got to the shack, Slim stormed inside to change his jeans, and he didn't invite us into the house.

We set up shop on the porch, right in front of the screen door. I scorched the runt with a glare. "How could you have done that? *How could you have done that!*"

He was almost in tears. "I don't know. He was so kind...and he rubbed me behind the ears...and I just melted inside."

"You melted, all right, and dumped five gallons of water in his lap!"

"I couldn't hold it!"

"Why didn't you move?"

"I don't know! I was sad and scared of being soup, then he rubbed my ears and I was so happy...oh, I've ruined everything! I'm such a failure!"

He broke down and started bawling, crying his little heart out. Tears dripped off his nose and plinked on the porch. And I had to watch and listen to the whole thing.

You know, those of us who go into Security Work have to be pretty hard-boiled, but there are times when our spirits are touched by the softer things in life. I felt a tug at the heart of my purse strings, and laid a paw upon his shoulder. "Okay, that's enough. Stop crying."

He shook his head. "I can't, I'm so ashamed!"

"Drover, if you'll stop crying, I'll tell you a deep dark secret."

He sniffled and looked at me through tear-shining eyes. "You will?"

"Yes. Come closer." I leaned into his ear and

whispered, "Half of that water was mine."

He let out a gasp. "No fooling? You did it too?"

"Shhh, not so loud. Yes, that's why the stain was so big. I don't know how it happened. It just slipped out, and if you ever breathe a word of this to anyone, I'll...I don't know what I'll do, but you won't like it."

All at once, he was laughing and hopping around. "Now I'm happy again! Hee hee! Thanks for telling me. Maybe I'm normal, after all."

"Don't get carried away. Slim doesn't know which one of us did it, but he's mad enough to bite nails. It's going to take some hard selling to get us into the house."

"Heavy Begs?"

"Exactly. Do you remember the protocol?"

He cocked his head to the side and stared at me. "I thought protocol was cough medicine."

"No, it's the procedure we follow: Sad Eyes, Lifeless Tail, Tragic Ears, Looks of Remorse, and lots of whimpering."

"Yeah, but my tail's too short to look lifeless."

"Good point. I'll handle the tail, you double up on the whimpering. But get this. We're going to make this presentation as a song. We will sing in a whimpering tone. Can you do it?"

He grinned. "Oh yeah, I'm ready to roll!"

"That's the spirit. Would you like to know the name of our song?"

"No, it might confuse me."

"Good point. Okay, let's set the formation." I put Drover on the right side of the screen door and I took the left side. On my signal, we launched our song. Here's how it went.

CHAPTER TEN

A Great Song

We Feel So Ashamed

We feel so ashamed.
We know we're to blame
For making that stain on your trousers.
We have no excuse.
Our water turned loose.
And now you must jump in the shower.

Our hearts are attacked.
We know you are hacked.
We really can't blame you for fuming.
But, Slim, there is really no point in this
   dooming and glooming.

It happened so fast
And now we're aghast
For hosing you down without warning.
We wet like a toad,
Your lap caught the load
And now we have gone into mourning.

We'd do anything
To take back the sting
Caused by venting our distended bladders.
The last thing we want is making you madder.

Your patience is worn,
Our friendship is torn,
And Drover and I are just wretched.
We beg one more chance.
If you want, we will dance,
Or throw an old sock and we'll fetch it.

This comes from the heart,
We're ready to start
All over with fresh new intentions.
But we're here on the porch, as though we'd
    been put in detention.

So let me suggest
We put it to rest.

I think we can find a way out:
Forget the whole thing, and let your dogs stay
   in the house.

What do you think? Awesome song, right? I agree.

I wasn't surprised that Slim ignored us. He knew we were out there, he could hear our pleas, but his heart had turned to stone, and he made us work for it.

And we did. After going through the entire Heavy Begs Protocol, we had to bring out one of our all-time best sellers: Moans and Groans. It's a toughie, but when we do it right, it works like a charm.

We were three minutes into M&G when he finally showed up at the door. His appearance was a little shocking. He had taken a bath and changed into shorts and a T-shirt, and his legs... well, they were as skinny as fence posts and exactly the color of mayonnaise. No kidding.

He leaned against the door jamb, crossed his arms, and glared down at us. "Am I going to have to listen to this mess all night long?"

Well, yes, if that's what it took.

"Y'all don't deserve a home that's clean and decent."

We held our breaths and waited.

"You ought to live outside with the toads and goats."

Boy, he was really pouring it on this time.

"If I was to let you inside, would I need to put you in diapers?"

Diapers! What a tacky thing to say. But you know what? He was beginning to loosen up.

He nudged the screen door with his toe and pushed it halfway open. "The first bonehead that wets on my floor..."

We didn't give him a chance to finish his threat. We shot the gap, squirted through the crack in the door, and took our places in the middle of the living room floor. There, we became Perfect Doggies. He raved on for another three minutes, but that was okay. When you win, you can put up with their raving.

At last, he wore himself out and flopped down in his big easy chair. He stared at the telephone on the floor. "I've got to call Viola, and I'm dreading it." He got up, paced around the house, ate a cracker, and returned to the chair. He took a deep breath, snatched up the phone, and dialed the number.

"Viola? Slim. Not so good. Viola, things are fixing to change over here." He told her about the

day's events: the drought, the fire, haystacks burned, shipping the cows to market, and his job ending in two days.

I couldn't hear her side of the conversation, but I had a pretty good idea how she took the news. Bad. She was fond of Slim, don't you see, and everybody in the neighborhood knew it, even the dogs. This was back before he gave her the lock-washer "engagement ring," and we all kept hoping that one day, he would open his eyes and...

I really don't want to get started on this, but I guess I will.

Okay, here we go. Slim had called Drover and me *boneheads*? Ha. He was the King of Boneheads! Miss Viola was the sweetest, kindest, prettiest lady in Texas. Furthermore, she was single and lived only three miles down the creek from Slim's shack. Three miles!

She had put out hints and given him opportunities, but here he was—still a dirty bachelor with mayonnaise legs, living alone in a shack, fixing to lose his job and move off to Montana...and miss out on the gift of a lifetime, a woman who might actually care about him!

Blind, that's what he was, blind, deaf and dumb, clueless, a perfect bonehead to the bitter end. And there wasn't one thing I could do about it.

Oh well, back to the phone conversation. "Anyway, Loper wondered if you could come over and ride with us day-after tomorrow. We'll be short-handed. Good. Six o'clock at the corrals. Thanks."

He hung up the phone and stared off into space. "That's one fine lady."

Yeah? Well, this was a great time for him to be figuring that out—now that he was fixing to leave the country, now that it was too late to do anything.

You know, I'd always felt a powerful friendship with this guy, but there were times when I thought he didn't deserve a patient, loyal dog. He needed a wolverine or a badger that would bite him three times a day. A pet shark. A snapping turtle.

There's a wise old saying about people who won't open their eyes and see what's right in front of them, but I'm so mad, I can't remember it.

Phooey.

Sorry I got carried away. Where were we? Oh yes.

Shipping Day started early. Slim was up at 4:30, made his coffee, and put on a fresh pair of jeans and a clean shirt. He pulled on his high-top riding boots with the spurs attached, fetched his chaps from the closet, and walked over to the door.

Did he say, "Good morning" or "Hello, dogs"? Oh no. He opened the door and grumbled, "Out." In the mornings, he has all the charm of a buzzard.

Out on the porch, he turned on his flashlight and stuck the light beam right into my eyes. "Ya'll ain't invited to this. Stay here."

Fine with me. Who wanted to spend another day with him anyway? The old grump.

On his way to the pickup-trailer rig, he looked up at the sky, a huge black dome lit up with a million stars. It was a desert sky: clear dry air and not a cloud in sight. I heard him mutter, "We sure won't need our slickers today. Elmer Kelton had it right: The Time It Never Rained."

He climbed into the pickup, cranked up the motor, turned on the lights, and drove away. Just for the record, his trailer lights blinked off and on, making it look like some kind of Christmas display. Faulty wiring. Typical cowboy rig.

You probably think that Drover and I spent the rest of the day sitting on the porch like stumps, snapping at flies and saying "Duhhh" to each other. Nope. I gave old Slimbo about thirty seconds of drive time, then turned to Drover.

"All right, men, it's time to move out."

He glanced around. "Move out of what?"

"They'll be loading trucks today and they can't do it without dogs. We're sending the entire Security Division to help."

"Yeah, but he told us to stay here."

"Drover, part of a dog's challenge in this life is figuring out which of their orders we should ignore. Let's go."

"Jump into the back of a moving pickup?"

"That's correct. We've done it before: Syruptishus Loaderation."

"Yeah, but..." He took a few limping steps and crashed. "Oh drat, there it went! This old leg just quit me."

I didn't have time to give him the tongue lashing he needed. "Fine, stay here and I'll load all the trucks myself, but this will go into my report."

As I dashed away from the porch, I heard his faint reply. "Oh, my leg! Oh, the guilt!"

How am I supposed to run a ranch when...oh well. He was no good at loading cattle anyway, the little weenie, because he was scared of getting kicked or stepped on. I would be better off without him.

I went racing after the pickup and leaped into the back. It wasn't so easy, because the pickup was pulling a gooseneck trailer. If a guy misses his jump or bangs his head against the neck of the trailer, he runs the risk of falling out of the pickup and getting run over.

A lot of dogs wouldn't have attempted such a foot...wouldn't have tempted their feet...the point is, I took a huge professional risk, disobeying an order and diving into the back of a moving pickup. It had nothing to do with Slim's charming personality, but had a lot to do with a cowdog's deep sense of loyalty to his outfit.

When they need us, we show up. When there's work to do, we're there.

Slim and Loper would be short-handed, and whether they knew it or not, they would need my help loading those trucks.

And then...well, there was Miss Viola. Don't forget, she was crazy about me, and I had a feeling that she would be very impressed when she saw me loading trucks. A guy should never pass up a chance to impress the ladies, right? You bet.

So there I was in the back of Slim's pickup. He turned right on the county road and drove the two miles to ranch headquarters. The lights were on in the house when we drove past, and through the windows, I saw Loper and Sally May getting ready for the big day that lay before them.

Even at a distance, I could see the sadness in their faces. This was the day of our Last Roundup.

CHAPTER ELEVEN

On the Long, Dusty Trail

Slim drove down to the corrals, turned off the engine and the lights, and started his morning chores. He fed the three horses he'd left up for the night: Dude for Loper, Snips for Slim, and Shadow, the Welsh pony, for Alfred. When the horses finished slobbering over their oats (they are such gluttons), he saddled them up.

Me? I laid low. If Slim had caught me in the back of his pickup, he would have thrown a fit and locked me in the saddle shed.

Along about six o'clock, when first light was showing on the eastern horizon, the others arrived: Loper, Sally May and Baby Molly, Alfred, and Miss Viola, with her sorrel mare in a two-horse side-by-side trailer.

It was a pretty solemn occasion and nobody was cracking jokes. Loper explained the plan. We would drive two pickups to the north end of the ranch and unload the horses. Sally May would drive the pickup, the one without the trailer, and honk the horn, calling the cows. She would drive slowly to the south, while the riders followed along, horseback, picking up strays and calves.

She would go through a wire gate into the next pasture, honking and calling the cows in that pasture too, and in the next pasture to the south. By the time we got to the headquarters corrals, we would have two hundred cows and about the same number of calves.

In an ordinary, good-grass year, this roundup strategy wouldn't have worked. We would have needed six cowboys to make the gather. You're probably wondering why it worked this time, and you asked the right dog.

See, in a drought, the cows are hungry. They've been scratching out a living on thistles, mesquite beans, gourd vines, and tree leaves, so when you blow the horn and rattle a feed sack, they'll follow you all the way to Brownsville. All you need is a few riders on the drag-end to sweep up the calves and keep the herd moving along.

It's pretty amazing that a dog would know so much about roundup strategy, isn't it? You bet. That's why they call us cowdogs instead of porch-dogs. We know our cows, and don't forget where Drover was spending his morning, the little slacker. On the porch of Slim's shack.

They loaded the four horses into the gooseneck trailer, and we left the corrals and drove north. Viola rode in the pickup with Sally May and the kids. Loper got in with Slim (I was in the back, but they didn't know it) and we made the slow three-mile drive over pasture trails to the north end of the ranch. It took us twenty minutes.

There, they unloaded the horses and the riders mounted up, just as pink light was beginning to show on the horizon. Loper glanced around to see that everyone was ready. "Well, this is a sad day for our family and this ranch. God bless us and keep us safe this morning...and send us a rain, even though it's too late."

Slim nodded. "Amen. Anybody heard a weather forecast?"

Loper flashed a bitter smile. "No, but it hasn't changed in six months: hot and dry, dry and hot, hotter and drier. Let's go." Sally May drove south and start blowing the horn, and the roundup began. Hungry cows came fogging out of the draws and canyons, and Sally May led the way.

I waited until they had gone a quarter-mile before I gave them the great news that I had come to help. Let's face it, early exposure could have gotten me locked in the stock trailer. It had happened before. I mean, those guys had some peculiar ideas about gathering cattle, and sometimes I got the feeling that...well, they just didn't understand how important it was to have a top-of-the line, blue-ribbon cowdog on the team.

Hard to believe, isn't it?

I tagged along at a distance, then gradually picked up the pace until I "just happened" to end up trotting along beside Miss Viola and her mare. She wore a flat-brimmed felt hat with a braided rawhide stampede string under her chin (to keep the hat from blowing off in the wind), a western shirt with flowers and bright colors, blue jeans, and red roper boots with a nice little pair of Wayne Paul spurs on the heels.

She looked so fresh and pretty, it made me gasp...and wonder if Slim's head was filled with cement. He was going to leave this girl and move to Montana? Sometimes... oh well, we won't get started on that.

I trotted along beside her and was gawking so hard, I ran smooth into a mesquite bush. I guess that's when she noticed me. She was surprised.

"Hank? Where did you come from?" She turned in the saddle and called out to Slim, who was across the herd on the other side. "Slim, I didn't know you brought Hank."

"Neither did I." He spurred his horse and loped over to us, and scorched me with his eyes. "Bozo. I told you to stay at the house."

Yes, well, he should have known that wasn't going to work.

He rolled his eyes and grumbled. "Don't chase the cattle, don't bark, and try to act your age, not your IQ. If you start a stampede..."

Miss Viola cut him off. "Oh, he'll be all right. I'll keep an eye on him."

See? What did I tell you? She was crazy about me.

Well, the morning that had been so pleasant at six o'clock got less pleasant as the hours passed. The sun grew warm, then hot. The wind picked up, the same cruel dry wind that had been thrashing us for months, only now it was heavy with the smell of burned grass and a cloud of dust kicked up by a herd of slow-moving cows.

At nine o'clock, we came to a windmill and Loper called a halt. We'd been on the trail for two and a half hours. The riders were getting a little saddle-weary, and the cattle were ready for a drink at the stock tank.

We gathered at the pickup and Sally May passed out breakfast burritos (she'd made them the night before) and cups of fresh, cool water. I happened to be sitting at the feet of Guess Who, and she happened to be standing off to the side, near Slim, and I heard part of their conversation.

"What will you do?"

He gave his head a shake. "I don't know, Viola. Every cow outfit from Kansas to Mexico is in this same drought. There's no cowboy jobs left, 'cause the cows have all gone to the sale barn, same as we're doing here." He took a bite of his burrito. "All I know to do is start driving north 'til I find green grass, and that's liable to be Nebraska or Montana."

"That's a long way from home."

"Yes ma'am, and if I thought about it long enough, I'd feel pretty blue. I'm trying not to think about it."

Their eyes met. He gave her a sad smile, and she answered with a sad smile.

When the cattle had watered and caught their wind, Loper gave the order to mount up. Sally May drove ahead in the pickup and the cows strung out in a long line behind her, throwing up a cloud of dust that varied in color from gray to brown. The wind was coming out of the south, so everyone at the back of the herd was eating dirt—Little Alfred, Viola, and me.

I couldn't help being proud of the boy. I mean, this was the same little stinkpot who had ruined his dad's birthday cake, but here he was, a little man, making a hand on a cattle drive. You could tell that he was getting tired and saddle sore, and his face looked like a Halloween mask (dust), but he didn't whine or complain, and he kept his little pony moving down the trail.

Just when you think these kids are about two-thirds worthless, they do something to fool you.

Me? I stayed at the back of the herd and kept the slackers moving, the old thin cows and the young calves that were starting to pant. When they got too far behind the herd, I trotted behind 'em and gave 'em a snap on the hocks. It worked slick.

Okay, there was one hateful old bat who took a dim view of me chewing on her ankles. She wheeled around and...well, tried to run a horn through my gizzard. It was a little embarrassing, to tell the truth. She chased me out of the herd and around in circles, whilst my friends on the cowboy crew whooped with laughter and yelled,

"Git 'er, Hankie, git 'er, boy!"

Not funny. I mean, the old hag wasn't kidding about this, and...never mind. I took my position at the back of the herd, next to a certain lady, and we resumed our slow march to headquarters.

On and on we went, through heat and dust. By the time we made it down the caprock and looked off into the valley below, we saw six big double-decker cattle trucks parked on the county road, waiting to load.

When we reached the road, Loper rode over to Cesar Rodriguez and shook his hand, wished him good morning and thanked him for being on time.

Then he gazed at that long line of trucks and... well, I guess it hit him for the first time that they were going to haul every cow he owned to the sale barn. In two hours, the ranch would be empty.

We bunched the herd in front of the corrals and started pushing them through the gate. In the past, we'd seen days when the cattle had given us trouble and had tried to stampede back to the pasture, but these cows were tired and thirsty, beat down from months of drought, and they didn't have any fight left in them.

They walked through the gate in a huge cloud of dust and stared at us with red, empty eyes.

After we'd penned the herd, we had to separate the cows and calves, and you probably wonder why, since sorting a big herd of cattle is a lot of trouble. The reason is that if you haul cows and calves in the same truck, some of the calves are liable to get stepped on by the cows. The calves might weigh only 300-400 pounds, don't you see, while a grown cow might weigh 1100-1200 pounds, and if you crowd 'em together in a tight space... you get the point.

So we separated the cows from the calves. It's called "cutting" cattle, and I happen to be very good at it. Some people think...

"Hank, get out of the gate!"

...that cutting has to be done horseback, but...

"Hank, go to the house!"

...but I can testify that horses don't know beans about cutting. It's a job for a top-of-the-line, blue-ribbon...

"Alfred, get your dog out of the pens!"

Huh?

Okay, sometimes the cowboys prefer doing their cutting horseback. It's slower and cruder than doing it with dogs, but...anyway, Alfred needed some company, so I, uh, joined him outside the corrals. There, we watched the action and choked on the dust, and I licked him on the cheek.

Pretty touching, huh? You bet. A boy and his dog, but no cake this time.

Oh, and here's a little detail I forgot to mention, a detail that nobody else noticed. After giving the lad's face a good washing, I happened to look up and saw something I hadn't seen in months.

Dark clouds in the sky.

CHAPTER TWELVE

A Change of Plans

The sorting took an hour—slow, hot work in a set of pens that hadn't seen a drop of rain in months. Every time an animal took a step, it created a puff of dust, and don't forget, we had four hundred cows and calves in the corral. When you multiply Puff x 400, you get a constant fog of dust, as well as red eyes, runny noses, and dirty faces. It was awful.

By the time the sorting was done, Cesar had backed his truck up to the loading chute and had opened up the compartments to receive the first bunch of cows. He stuck his head out the trailer door and called out the numbers he wanted: "Five, twenty, twenty, and five!"

That was my signal to spring into action. We

were ready to load. I left Alfred, sprinted across the corral, wiggled under two fences, and took up my position outside the crowding alley. I turned toward the riders and barked the orders. "Okay, we're ready to load. Bring five head!"

This was going to be a big job and somebody needed to take charge.

Loper, Slim, and Viola spurred their weary horses, cut off five cows, and drove them into the crowding alley. I took over from there. Darting my head through the spaces between the boards in the fence, I chewed hocks, snarled, snapped, and barked the cows up the loading chute and into the truck.

Cesar closed a compartment door inside the cattle trailer and yelled, "Twenty!" I turned to the riders and relayed the orders. "Bring twenty head, and let's not have any fooling around!"

Here they came, twenty head, each with four legs, which meant that I had a total of eighty ankles to bite. Huge job. No ordinary dog could have...

Rain drop?

No ordinary dog could have done it. Did you notice that rain drop? Maybe not, since you weren't there, but I noticed. It was a big one and it splattered right on the end of my nose. Several more landed in the pen and, oddly enough, they kicked up little puffs of dust.

Loper gazed up at the sky but went right on with the work. I mean, getting a few counterfeit drops of rain was nothing new to this outfit. It had been going on for months and we'd seen it all before: clouds moved in, bunched together, built up into towering thunderheads, kicked out a few pitiful drops of rain, and fell apart, leaving hearts broken and expectations crushed.

Nobody on our outfit was going to fall for that trick. We kept working. "Twenty cows!" They brought the cattle, pushed them into the crowding pen, and closed the gate, and I took over from there.

"Up the chute, you codfish! Load up, you're going to town!"

Boy, you should have seen me in action! Bite, bark, snap, and snarl, what a piece of work it was, and I hardly noticed the rain drops. More than one. More than ten. Quite a few, actually, but we'd been to this rodeo before and nobody on our crew was going to play the fool—*because we no longer believed in rain.* It was all a big cruel joke.

"Five head!"

They brought the cattle and I barked 'em up the chute and into the truck. Cesar was right there, straddling the loading chute, and he jumped down and closed the sliding door. He grinned at me and winked. "Nice work, Lassie."

Who? Oh, maybe it was a joke. No problem. But he was right about the nice work. By George, we had turned in a pretty slick piece of...a cold blast of wind sent cottonwood leaves clattering across the pen.

Cesar shielded his eyes with a hand and looked off to the northwest. "Holy cow, is that rain?" He cupped his hand and yelled, "Loper, we're fixing to get wet!"

Loper snorted at that. "We're fixing to get some wind. Let's load trucks!"

Cesar jumped into the cab of his Peterbilt and pulled away from the loading chute, just as the second truck came down the hill towards the pens. The two trucks had just passed each other...when it hit.

I could hear it coming, a roaring sound off to the northwest. I turned to look and watched as parts of the ranch began to disappear behind a veil of...surely that wasn't rain. We didn't believe in rain, right?

You know, one thing I've learned about rain is that it really doesn't care what you believe. And fellers, we got plastered. Forget the raindrops, this was buckets, driven by a wind that tore limbs off of trees.

What a crazy world. Five minutes earlier, we had been blinded by dust. Now we were blinded by water. The cattle turned their backs to the wind, dropped their heads, and dripped streams of water off their noses and tails.

Loper, the guy who didn't believe in rain, lost his hat and almost lost his horse when Dude got beaned on the head by a hailstone. Loper bailed out of the saddle and yelled, "It'll pass in five minutes, but we'd better take cover."

I don't know who or whom he was yelling at, 'cause the rest of us were already heading for cover under the calf shed. I was there when Slim and Viola arrived, leading their horses. Viola dived under the shed, while Slim went to work, jerking cinches and pulling saddles and bridles. He had to leave the horses out in the rain, don't you see, and didn't want the saddles to get soaked.

By the time he got that done, his shirt was plastered against his skin and his straw hat had taken on the shape of...I don't know, it resembled a chicken with its wings hanging down, and he looked pretty silly.

The rain roared on the tin roof. Little rivers of water ran through the corrals, floating dried cow chips that had been there since last fall. I had no idea where the rest of the crew had gone: Loper, Sally May, Baby Molly and Little Alfred. It was every man for himself, and we were all taking shelter wherever we could.

Over the drum of the rain, Viola yelled, "Will this end the drought?"

Slim's glasses were so wet and fogged, he couldn't see beans. He yelled, "This won't last long. It's the pattern in a drought. In fifteen minutes, the sun'll pop out and it'll be hotter than a skillet."

"Well, I'm freezing!"

Slim's face went blank for a moment, then he reached his arm across her shoulder and pulled her close. "Well, I'm warmer than a wet shirt."

"Really? I've wondered about that."

"What?"

"Nothing."

So there we stood, under the shed whose roof was gushing sheets of water, and waited for the rain to quit, just as we knew it would. It kept raining. The wind died down but the rain continued in a steady pour.

Fifteen minutes later, Loper came splashing through the corrals. He'd found a yellow rain slicker in the saddle shed and it had about fifteen mouse holes in it. His hat was a ruin and his hair hung down in his eyes.

"Cesar's stuck in the mud and can't get his truck up the hill. We'd better get the tractor."

Slim rolled his eyes and shook his head. "Hey Loper, I know you don't want to believe this, but it's raining. Them ain't bird feathers falling out of the sky. Even if we pull him up the hill, he'll still have seven miles of muddy road before he gets to the blacktop."

Loper set his jaw. "We're shipping cattle. Come on."

He went back out in the rain. Slim shook his head and grinned at Viola. "He won't rest until we tear up some equipment. I'll see you later at the house...if I survive."

He trotted out into the rain. I was very tempted to stay behind with...well, You Know Who, but if my guys were fixing to tear up some equipment, I needed to be there to cheer them on. I dashed out into the rain and followed Slim up to the machine shed.

The John Deere tractor hadn't been driven in two months and had a mouse nest in the exhaust pipe. It caught fire and blew sparks all over the place, but since the air was as humid as a wet rag, the place didn't burn down.

Loper grabbed a big nylon tow rope and Slim drove the tractor to the base of the hill where Cesar was stuck. The tractor didn't have a cab, by the way, so he got even more soaked than he'd been before, and he could hardly see. The tractor slid in the mud and banged into the front bumper of the truck.

He yelled at Loper, "What did I tell you!" Loper, who looked like a drownded rat, ignored him. He hooked one end of the rope to Cesar's bumper and the other to the tractor. "Take 'er up the hill!"

Slim throttled up, shifted into first gear, and hit the end of the rope. It was nylon, so it stretched. The tractor tires ran like a buzz saw, slinging mud all over Slim and Loper. Cesar gunned the motor in the Pete...and guess what happened.

The rope broke, the truck slid into the ditch, and Slim and the tractor went flying off the side of the little hill and landed at the bottom.

Wow. In no time at all, they had stuck the tractor, stuck the truck, and broken a brand new nylon tow rope.

And the rain was still coming down in buckets. Slim came slipping and sliding up the hill— soaked, covered with mudballs, and mad. He was about to scream something, but Loper raised his hand for silence. "You were right, so dry up. Get Cesar and let's go to the house. Maybe Sally May can brew up some hot chocolate."

Slim glared at him, but finally grinned and muttered, "Loper, you're a piece of work, I'll swan."

Cesar left his truck in the ditch and we all trotted to the house. The men were in ruins—soaked from head to toe, limp hats, muddy boots, smelly, the whole nine yards of playing trucks and tractors in a pouring rain—so they didn't go inside the house. They pulled up lawn chairs and sat on the front porch.

And guess who was right there beside them to place his head in their laps and share his wet-dog aroma. Me.

Moments after they had settled into their chairs and propped their muddy boots on the porch rail, Loper grumbled, "Enjoy it while you can, boys, because it won't last five minutes."

Two hours later, we were still sitting on the porch, watching the rain. The guys had finished two cups of hot chocolate and Slim dashed across the yard to check the rain gauge. Five inches. When he got back, he said, "Well, what are you going to do with your cows?"

Loper shrugged. "We can't fight nature."

"Sure we can. You do it all the time. We've still got a couple of pickups that ain't stuck or tore up. Don't let a little rain ruin your plans."

Loper managed a chuckle. "If you ever move to Montana, I'll miss your warped sense of humor." He turned to Cesar. "Can we jump those cows out of the truck or will we need a portable loading chute? And by the way, we don't have a portable loading chute."

Cesar laughed. "They'll jump. I've done it before."

"Well, let's open the gates and turn 'em out. I hate to be a sucker for good news, but it looks like this rain has broken the drought. And thank you, Lord."

We opened all the gates and let a bunch of tired, hungry cows go looking for green grass.

Out in the Wild West, where we live, a five-inch rain brings everything to a dead stop. Parts of our roads got washed out and the rest became a swamp of mud, which meant that everybody associated with this deal was stranded at headquarters. I mean, you talk about muddy roads! Cesar and the drivers had to spend the night in their trucks and Miss Viola slept in Alfred's room. Slim, Alfred, and I camped on the porch and listened to the rain. What a great sound!

So there you are. The Last Roundup turned out to be a complete disaster, and we were all so happy, we could hardly sit still. The ranch survived the drought and Slim didn't have to move away.

Best of all, Sally May's rotten little cat got drenched and yowled all night long. Hee hee! I loved it, and what a wonderful way to finish the story!

This case is...oh, by the way, while the guys and I were sitting out on the porch, Sally May and Viola baked a birthday cake for Loper. The bad news is that I didn't get any of it.

Oh well, this case is closed.

Have you read all
of Hank's adventures?

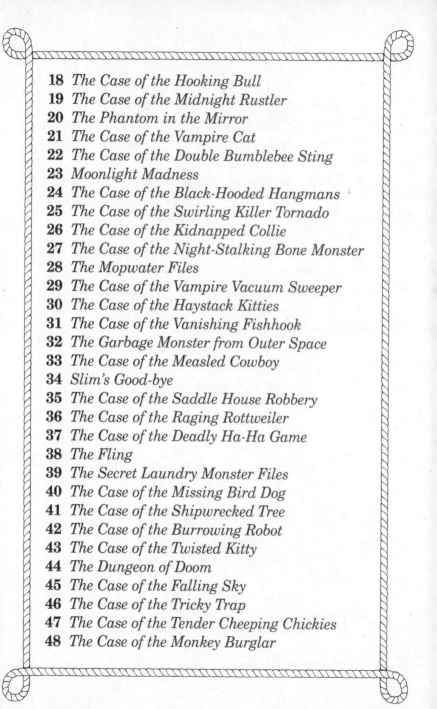

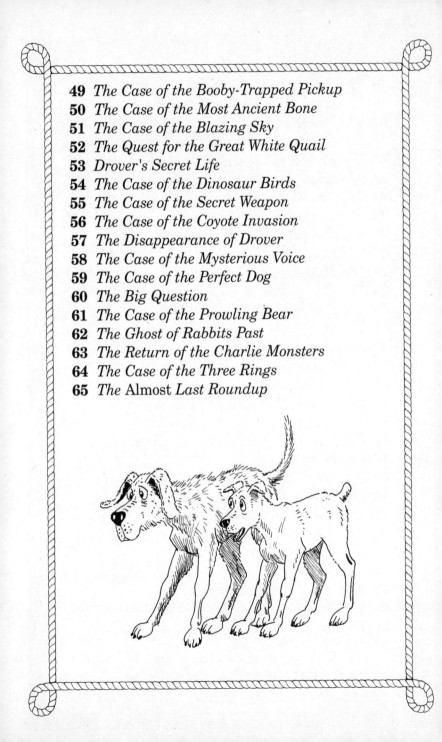

☐ Yes I want to join Hank's Security Force. Enclosed
   is $12.99 ($7.99 + $5.00 for shipping and handling)
   for my **two-year membership**. [Make check pay-
   able to Maverick Books.]

Which book would you like to receive in your Welcome Package?　　(#　　　)　any book except #50

BOY　or　GIRL

YOUR NAME
_____ (CIRCLE ONE)

MAILING ADDRESS
_____

CITY _____ STATE _____ ZIP _____

TELEPHONE _____ BIRTH DATE _____

E-MAIL　(required for digital Hank Times)

Send check or money order
for $12.99 to:

Hank's Security Force
Maverick Books
PO Box 549
Perryton, Texas 79070

DO NOT SEND CASH. NO CREDIT CARDS ACCEPTED.
Allow 2–3 weeks for delivery.
Offer is subject to change.

The following activity is a sample from *The Hank Times*, the official newspaper of Hank's Security Force. Please do not write on this page unless this is your book. Even then, why not just find a scrap of paper?

For more games and activities like these, as well as up-to-date news about upcoming Hank books, be sure to check out Hank's official website at **www.hankthecowdog.com**!

"Photogenic" Memory Quiz

We all know that Hank has a "photogenic" memory—being aware of your surroundings is an important quality for a Head of Ranch Security. Now you can test your powers of observation.

How good is your memory? Look at the illustration on page 99 and try to remember as many things about it as possible. Then turn back to this page and see how many questions you can answer.

1. Was Slim's chin on his Left or Right hand?

2. Was the picture frame a Rectangle, Oval, Square, or Triangle?

3. Does the phone plug in to the wall on the Left or the Right of the illustration?

4. Does the top part of the fridge start Above or Below Slim's eyes?

5. Was Hank looking to his Left or Right?

6. How many of Slim's toes could you see? 3, 4, 5, 10, or 15?

"Rhyme Time"

If the rain hadn't come, and Loper **had** had to sell the herd, what sorts of jobs could a cow get?

Make a rhyme using the word **COW** that would relate to a cow's new job possibilities below:

1. The cow becomes someone's pet cat.

2. The cow teaches court manners and what to do when you meet a King or Queen.

3. The cow starts a travel service featuring vacations to Hawaii.

4. The cow takes a hint from pet food and invents a food mix for cows.

5. The cow makes a toy gun.

6. The cow starts a farm and gets the ground ready to plant.

7. The cow becomes a preacher who performs marriages.

8. The cow teaches people how to live in the present.

9. The cow starts a first aid business.

10. The cow moves to Russia and lives there.

Answers:

1. Cow MEOW
2. Cow BOW
3. Cow LUAU
4. Cow CHOW
5. Cow POW
6. Cow PLOW
7. Cow VOW
8. Cow NOW
9. Cow OW
10. Cow MOSCOW

Photo Courtesy of Western Horseman Magazine

John R. Erickson, a former cowboy, has written numerous books for both children and adults and is best known for his acclaimed *Hank the Cowdog* series. He lives and works on his ranch in Perryton, Texas, with his family.

Gerald L. Holmes has illustrated numerous cartoons and textbooks in addition to the *Hank the Cowdog* series. He lives in Perryton, Texas.

Shawn Tevis Photography